The Set Up

Triplets: Three Aren't One

Book One

by

Dani Haviland

USA Today Bestselling Author

The Set Up and *Triplets: Three Aren't One* are works of fiction. Names, place, characters, and incidents are the product of the author's imagination and are used for the readers' enjoyment. Any resemblance to persons living, dead, or fictional, events or business establishments is entirely coincidental.

Book Description

Just before high school graduation, life seemed perfect. Grace is suddenly knocked into a harsh reality by her manipulative mother who demands absolute obedience. Everything changes when the three Armstrong brothers come into her life.
Will she ever get back to her one true love?
And will he want her again if he finds out what she's done?

Praise and Awards

USA Today Bestselling Author

Kindle Top 100 Bestselling Author

Amazon Top 100 Historical fiction Author

Amazon Top 100 Biographies and Memoirs Author

Amazon Top 100 Short Story Anthologies and Collections

Amazon Top 100 History of Women in the American Civil War

Amazon Top 100 United States Drama and Plays

Amazon Top 100 LGBT Mysteries Author

Amazon Top 100 Weddings

Amazon Top 100 Satire

"There wasn't a heartstring this one didn't pull at! And, no spoilers, but that's one of the nicest endings I could have imagined – all round, proving redemption's possible, some things will last forever, and .... Karma. This isn't just a story of Jose and Loren; it's so much more.

Amazon reader on *Too Fast for You*

"From the picturesque descriptions of the Alaskan wilderness, to weaving a beautiful love story, the author's writing style is both serious and quirky. A perfect, relaxing read!"

Amazon review of *One Arctic Summer*

Chapter 1
Mother Knows Best

May 15, 1991

"Are you sure we should be doing this?" Dusty asked breathlessly.

With hormone-induced strength and determination, Grace wrapped her fingers around his and pried his protective hand away from his half-unbuttoned fly. "Yes, I'm sure," she cooed seductively.

"But…but…what if you get pregnant?" he whispered. "Can't you just do the grab and tug thing again?"

"You may like that, but it doesn't do a thing for me except give me sticky fingers. And not the good kind like after eating a giant cinnamon roll with extra glaze. Now, come on! We're both old enough now. At eighteen, no one can say anything." Grace tucked her fallen hair behind her ear and straightened her shoulders. "We're consenting adults."

"But…but… Oh, man…" Dusty slumped back into the couch cushions, defeated in his battle to keep her virginity intact. His virginity, too. He was about to be both a winner and a loser in the battle of fear of and desire for the greatest treasure the human body had to offer.

Grace pulled her tank top off over her head, then shimmied out of her jeans, standing before him: the goddess of female perfection in lace and lust. "You still have that condom, don't you? I think you've been carrying that around since you were thirteen!"

"Oh, yeah…" Dusty reached into his hip pocket and pulled out his wallet. He fumbled through his single dollar bills until he found it. Hastily, he tore open the pale blue packet, then moaned as it fell apart in his fingers.

Tears welled up in his eyes as he looked up to her.

"What?" she asked. She took it from him and held it under the lamp on the end table. "Oh, shit!" She huffed and grunted in frustration, then looked up to see his reaction.

Eyes red with stifled tears, Dusty wiped under his nose, trying to compose himself. His emotions had fallen apart, but the message hadn't been relayed to his male member, still hard and ready to procreate.

Grace gently touched the firmness in his red knit boxer shorts, so different now that she knew it was about to be hers. She leaned over and whispered, "Don't worry. I'm a virgin, so since it's the first time, I can't get pregnant." She took in the size of his erection — longer than the length of her hand — and winced, a slight groan escaping. "At least, that's what Shawna said. Plus, just to make sure, you can pull out at the last minute or second or whatever. Shawna said it's messy, but she's had sex lots of times and she's not pregnant."

"Well, if you're sure…" Dusty rolled sideways and sat up, fumbling with his jeans. "I'll do this part. I know zippers are easier for you, but I didn't think we were going to be doing anything like this tonight." He stopped at the last button. "Are you sure your parents are gone for the whole weekend?"

Grace leaned against the wall, watching the awkward striptease by the young man who had fascinated her since he had started working with his father as a groundskeeper. Dusty was still gawky and lean but had the broadest shoulders of any man she'd ever seen without wearing full football regalia. He didn't play for her school, but she didn't care. That just meant he wasn't stuck on himself like the guys at her private academy.

"Um…" Dusty paused and looked around the guest house living room that doubled as the game room. "Aren't we supposed to have a bed or something? I really don't know what I'm doing here."

"We'll figure it out. At least we're not in the back of a car. You're not only my best guy friend," Grace said, shaking from both the chilly air and nerves, "you're my first lover."

Dusty stepped on the hem of the pant leg still tangled around his ankle. "And your last lover, too," he added hastily and lifted his leg up, nearly toppling over. "Because I don't ever want to lose you."

Grace moved to his side quickly, shoring him up. "Kind of hard to lose someone who never wants to leave your side." She glanced down and saw he was still ready for her. "Or your front," she added with a giggle.

"You know, there's no reason to rush into this…"

"Dusty, I've been waiting for two years, at least!" Grace reached around and unhooked her bra, freeing her perky breasts that didn't really need a brassiere. "Tonight's the first time we've been alone together, and I want you bad! I mean, I want you good. Or want you great. Oh, hell!"

Grace tossed her bra onto the couch and wrapped both arms around her sinewy wannabe lover, rubbing her belly against his, feeling with her abdomen what she had only touched with her hands. "Couch?" she panted.

"Oh, yeah…"

The teenage couple stumbled to the green damask-covered sofa, arms and legs bumping into each other as throw pillows were tossed aside, fingers fumbling to grab body parts and place them where their overstimulated hormones directed.

"Oh, man," Dusty groaned, submitting to her climbing on top of his naked body. She scooted forward, trying to find a place to set her knee in the couch. Making the most out of the awkward situation, she bent forward and kissed him as she reached back to find his cock. She rubbed it against the fuzziness of her pubic hair and tried to straddle him.

"I don't think I can stop…" he moaned as his back arched, trying to penetrate her.

"Then don't," she whispered.

"Huh?" he asked, paralyzed in fear that she had changed her mind.

"Don't stop, I mean. Please." She found her moist opening and gently sat back on his dick, wiggling to get it in all the way. "I want you so bad I ache!"

Dusty pushed up further, eliciting a squeak from his partner. "Does it hurt?" he asked, pausing.

"No. I…I…" She lifted her hips and came back down on him, slowly, then lifted up again, her lady muscles automatically squeezing as she moved up, relaxing as she sat back down. "Oh, man…"

The two quickly found their rhythm. "Oh, oh, oh!" Grace squealed as an orgasm approached.

"Should I stop?" he asked.

She squirmed on top of him, enjoying her last shudder, then sighed in completion. "Not yet, but let's change places."

The two disengaged and Dusty climbed on top. They started again slowly, the music on the CD player setting them up with a new pace. Gradually, their movements increased to a drum roll speed, the rock tune unheard. Suddenly, he paused, eyes wide in shock.

"Ah, shit!" he shrieked and quickly pulled out, squirting his load on the couch.

"Huh?" she asked, confused at the abrupt loss of physical contact.

"Babies," he panted. "Not today, I hope."

"Oh, yeah. I forgot."

"I'm glad I didn't. Just a sec." Dusty stood up and retrieved his boxers from the pile of abandoned clothing. "I'll clean this up." He wiped the spilled seed from between her legs. *Let's hope the coach was wrong. He said whenever you have sex could be the time you make a baby. I guess I shouldn't tell her that word is that Shawna's already had two abortions.*

"Um, can we do it again? I mean, I thought it was going to hurt the first time."

"For me or for you?" Dusty asked. "Because it sure didn't hurt me!"

"For me. I guess that time I fell on my cousin's bike rail did make a difference. I remember my mom saying something about how it popped my cherry."

"Huh?"

"That virgin piece that gets in the way and is pierced the first time a woman has sex. I think it's called the hymen or hybrid or something like that. Anyhow, I broke it when I was six. I remember when it happened, it hurt like I'd been slammed down there with a hammer. I bled, too. It stopped hurting a few hours later, though. I guess it was a small sacrifice. Oh, and hey! I think I had my first orgasm."

"Really? What was it like?" Dusty asked, grateful for the pause in activities so he could recover.

"Um, you know how when you ride on the Ferris wheel you get all tingly down *there*?"

"Oh, yeah. I thought only guys got that. I mean, it can give a guy a boner if he's not careful."

Grace giggled at the word boner, then composed herself. "So, did you have an orgasm, too?"

"Well, with a guy it's different. There's a visible spurt when he has one. Kind of hard to fake." He held up the shorts he'd used as a washcloth. "Proof positive."

"Keep that close at hand," she said. "I think we'll need to use it at least once more. Sex is fun. Now I know why everyone likes it so much."

"Anything for you, Gracie. Anything."

***

"Oh, shoot! Look at the time! I gotta get home or my dad will clobber me. We have to start work at six tomorrow. I hope I can sneak in without him seeing me."

Grace rolled off his outstretched arm. "It's three o'clock? Yeah,

I guess I'd better get busy and clean up this place. I don't think my folks will be back until tonight, but I was supposed to be staying with Shawna. We kinda-sorta made a mess in here."

The two cuddled close to each other on the couch, their eyes following the trail of clothes and scattered magazines from the coffee table, the pool cues and chalk now on the floor, the pool table cover wadded into a pillow on top of their impromptu bed.

"I'll never forget this night," Dusty said and stood up. "But I really have to leave. You're okay with cleaning this up by yourself?"

"Pbbt! Of course I am." She got up and turned her face into his chest, giving him a quick kiss on his sparse chest hairs, inhaling deeply to memorize his musky scent. "Give me a call later if you can."

"I'll do better than that. If we finish early, I'll drop by and see you. But I can't get done early if I don't make a good showing for the old man." Dusty stepped into his jeans and quickly jumped up twice to get them all the way on.

Giggling behind her hand at his male parts bouncing with the quick-dress movement, Grace suddenly remembered his skivvies. She looked over at the very well-used cleanup cloth. "Um, I think you forgot something…"

His face brightened red in embarrassment. "Just throw them away. The next time, I'll make sure we have something more suitable."

"Ah," Gracie sighed, her hand brought up to caress her breast in recall. "The next time."

Dusty pulled his tee-shirt on over his head, grabbed his socks from the floor and stuffed them in his pants pocket, then stepped into his tennis shoes. He gave her a quick kiss, groaned, then bent in to embrace her with a full-body hug and smooch. "I can't wait to have you every morning, noon, and night for the rest of my life. But it's going to have to wait. I really do love you, you know."

"Yeah, me too," Grace said. "On everything." She patted him

on the shoulder and urged him to the door. "Go. Now. If you don't, I won't let you out of my sight again. Ever."

"All right. Tonight if I can. And if I can't, I'll find a way."

"Find a way…" Grace said, and moved him out the door, shutting and deadbolting it behind him. "Because I'll be waiting," she said to herself softly. She looked at the daunting task of cleaning up the normally tidy room, then decided it could wait a few hours. She picked up one of the throw pillows from the floor and cuddled up with it on the couch. "I can't imagine life without you now."

***

"What in the hell happened in here?"

Grace awoke disoriented, her mother's shrill voice like tiny knives in her head, trying to carve their way out of her brain through her ears. She shook her head, struggling to remember where and who she was.

"Well? Answer me!"

Still clutching the pillow close, Grace realized she was naked, in a room not her own, and her mother was back almost a day earlier than planned. The first two dilemmas weren't as bad as the last one. If Mother was home early, that meant her parents had had another major blow-up. Would Dad finally get fed up and leave? And if he did, where would she go? She still had two weeks of school left until she graduated.

Grace felt her mother's cold, bony hand grab her chin, bringing her out of her daze. "I asked you," she said icily, her eyes piercing, looking for the telltale signs of lying. "What happened here?"

"I didn't want to go to Shawna's," she said honestly, hoping her talent for storytelling was wide awake and creative. "I put on some loud music, shot pool until three in the morning, then got tired." *All true except I used the pool table for a different purpose.*

"And your clothes…"

"Bra was too tight after binging on chips and soda. Plus, it was hot." Grace quickly scanned the room, looking for more fodder for her fabrication. "You know, you really ought to have that handyman check out the heating and cooling system in here. One minute, everything's fine; the next minute, I'm sweating like a boxer."

And then she saw them, lying next to the trash can she had thrown them at and missed. Grace quickly looked away and focused on the pool table, hoping her mother hadn't followed her gaze to see Dusty's left-behind red underwear.

"Speaking of boxers," her mother said. She walked over and kicked at the wadded shorts. She noticed the stiff and shiny spots where body fluids had dried and her blood pressure skyrocketed. "It looks like you had company," she said through clenched teeth.

"What are those doing there?" Grace asked, trying to look shocked rather than embarrassed. *Yeah, what are those doing there? They should have made it to the bottom of the trash, at least!*

"I don't know what I did to have such an ungrateful daughter. I put up with your father's pawing and whining just so you can have a nice home and the finer things in life. A home to be proud of, not to bring horny boys to for a good time. How many times? How long has this been going on?" Victoria asked, her nails digging in as she clenched her daughter's upper arm. "It was that gardener's kid, wasn't it?"

"Let go! You're hurting me," Grace yelped, shoulder dipping as she tried to twist out of her mother's angry grasp. She knew it was useless, though. Her mother always got to have her own way through intimidation and, lately, her physical prowess. All those hours she spent at the gym were good for more than sporting the tightest abs and best-toned legs of any woman in her forties. She could twist the freckles off a frog if she had a mind to.

Grace had made her mother angry many times in the past but this time, she was livid. Was it because sex was involved or had she had a spectacularly horrid time with Dad and come back early, ready to blame someone – anyone –for her miserable existence? This time, Mother hadn't even tried to lecture her. She had gone straight to screaming and grabbing.

Slap!

"What was that for?" Grace asked, her hand up to cover her stinging cheek.

"Who was it? No, never mind. I'm pretty sure it was that lowlife without prospects for a decent future." Victoria paced the room, walking and plotting, pausing to snort in indignation, then stopped suddenly. Her eyes brightened and a conniving smile spread across her face as she realized she could still make this work in her favor. Grace had just sped up the time frame. Her daughter would just have to skip college and go straight to a well-contrived marriage. She had saved the family a fortune in tuition, sorority fees, living expenses and probably a trip to Europe or two.

Grace watched her mother pace but didn't engage her. Instead, she stooped to pick up her clothes and got dressed, stealing sidelong glances to keep track of the mercurial moods. She had just set the pool table straight when she saw Mother's devilish smirk appear. *Crap!*

"I guess this situation is still salvageable, but you're going to have to do everything I say." She looked at Grace and saw her cheek was still crimson from being slapped. She hadn't done that in ages. She didn't regret it but did feel bad that it would probably leave a mark for more than an hour.

"Sorry about that," Victoria said, trying for sincerity but knowing Grace could see right through her. "I kind of lost my cool when I found out you'd been sleeping around. I guess it doesn't make a difference how many times you've done it or with whom. What you need to do now is find a Mr. Right who has a brother. I want you to sleep with both of them. It'd be better if we can find a family with three available brothers."

"What are you babbling about?"

"Three brothers and who cares if one, or even two, are married? As long as one is single so you can marry him. Actually, multiples might be better. Throw in a little family drama and we might get a six-figure buyout. If you're pregnant, eh? We'll deal with that later."

"I'm not pregnant," Grace said. "We were careful. And I don't want to sleep around. I want to marry Du…"

Grace's eyes widened, shocked that her mother's hand was on her face again. This time, it wasn't a slap, but a firm grip over her mouth to keep her from speaking.

"You will do as I say," Victoria said, glaring at her daughter. "I didn't want to have you to begin with, but you did give me a comfortable existence for the past nineteen years. If you don't do as I say, I will have your little boyfriend arrested for rape."

Grace twisted her head and escaped her mother's grasp. "I'm eighteen and you know it! He is, too. There's no way…"

Humph!

Grace doubled over with the punch to the gut, then looked up, shocked and amazed at the new level of physical violence her mother had sunk to. "What? Why?" she gasped.

"Birth certificates are so easy to fake. All I have to do is make a few calls and the police will be out here, looking for the man who raped my seventeen-year-old daughter."

"But it wasn't…"

Fwap! Thunk!

Two more punches – one to the face, another to the belly – and Grace was on the floor.

"Care for a few more?" her mother asked snidely. "If you give in now and do as I say, he won't be arrested for rape, assault with intent to kill, robbery… Give me a minute and I can think of a few more charges. Looks like I have corroborating evidence on who the culprit was, too." Victoria grabbed one of the pool cues and lifted up the underwear loaded with DNA samples.

Grace remained on the carpet to avoid more of her mother's painful blows, considering her options as she held her pain and rage in check with the slow, steady breathing techniques she had learned in yoga classes.

If I play along, Dusty will be safe. Whether I have to be the docile daughter for a week, a month, or a year, it's still better than losing the love of my life to prison. Even if I can convince a judge that it wasn't rape and he isn't convicted, just being charged will smear his – our – life with a record.

Victoria watched as her daughter considered her choices. She knew she had brought up a smart girl who would come to the right conclusion. Still, a few pugilistic blows would show the little rebel that Mother was still bigger, stronger, and more determined to control a situation than she could ever be.

"Yes, do as I say," Victoria said using her low and sultry no-nonsense voice, "and both lover boy's record and your reputation will remain clean. No matter how innocent a girl is when she's 'taken advantage of,' having that event in her life will always be a stigma. You will be marked as that beautiful blonde who allowed herself to be raped.

"I also want you to consider what this would do to your father and his business if this debacle ever became known. Your name spread all over the newspapers, his clients avoiding the man whose daughter was violated. One look at your pretty little boyfriend, and they'll think you either lured him in or lied about the rape. Either way, everyone loses."

"And your way?" Grace asked, sniffing back her tears, hoping they weren't visible or were thought to be from the physical pain, not the loss of the life she had hoped for.

"You target a well-to-do young man and his brother. Or brothers. I'll help scout out the right ones. All you have to do is be pretty and make yourself available. Once you get one brother's interest, flirt with the other or others. Figure out which one you want to marry and you're set. Oh, and I don't care how 'careful' you were, the women in my family are extremely fertile. Unless you went behind my back and got an IUD or are on the pill, you're probably already pregnant."

"Why brothers?" Grace asked, forgoing a conversation on her level of fertility or method of contraception.

"Why not? Increase your chances of getting a better provider. Oh, and you have to sleep with both of them within the first week or two. It's leverage for the future. You may not ever need to use that secret against either one of them but consider it an insurance policy. No condoms, either. If you have sex with the brothers in the first month, you'll be pregnant and guaranteed a hurry-up wedding."

Victoria reached her hand out to help Grace from the floor, her fake smile not even beginning to cover her sneer of disgust. "It was bound to happen one way or another. You blew your chance at four years at an Ivy League college, scouting for Mr. Right. You'll have to settle for four weeks of hoping for a not-too-disgusting Mr. Right Now."

Grace rolled to her side and got up from the floor without assistance, ignoring her mother's hand. "If you don't mind, I'll finish cleaning up in here. Then I want to take a shower."

"You can scrub until sunset but the stink of messing up your life with a night of legs spread for the wrong man will never leave. We'll just have to make sure your Mr. Right Now is the same height and coloring as that gardener's son you've been drooling over for the last three years. At least you succumbed to someone of the right color."

Grace used every ounce of control – and the recent memory of being pummeled by the woman who claimed to love her – to keep from pivoting in place and spearing her mother with the pool cue she had just picked up. Instead, she bent over and gathered a fallen cube of cue chalk, crushing it between her thumb and fingers before dumping the clumpy blue powder into the trash. *One day at a time. One second at a time. Don't stoop to her level of assaulting from anger. Make a plan and keep to it. Protecting Dusty is worth it.*

Chapter 2

Surviving the Day

How could life have been so perfect at three in the morning and not worth living four hours later?

Grace rinsed the last of the shampoo from her hair, then watched as the bubbles slipped down the drain, disappearing into the blackness of the unknown just like her life. She tapped the stopper with her foot, allowing the tub to start filling. Mother said she wanted to talk when she was done but hadn't given her a deadline. She'd take every bit of time she could and give herself the full treatment including a hair masque and a few minutes with the jacuzzi. She patted herself gently between her legs. The swelling had gone down, but she was still tender. She'd set the jets on low for now.

A warm, comforting tingle ran up her spine at the memory of how she had become sore and how she had sprinted into womanhood, sharing her body and soul with the man she had chosen to spend forever with. Her smile and glow suddenly evaporated as a stream of water from the showerhead hit her cheek just wrong. She flinched at the pain, a reminder of her mother's harsh slap.

Why had that vile woman who birthed her dash her hopes and plans, sealing her dissertation with a one-two punch and a non-negotiable threat? Was it jealousy at her fading beauty or rage at her own failed marital relationship?

Grace turned off the shower and let the tub fill from the waterspout, the flow not too hot but warm enough to keep her from getting chilled. She squirted hair conditioner into the palm of her hand and new memories of the passions of the night before flooded in at the sight of the white creamy fluid. A shudder of mixed emotions – the recall of pleasure with and the despair at the loss of – Dusty overwhelmed her. She mindlessly applied the conditioner to the ends of her long hair, twisting the dark blonde tresses together, pressing the mass close to her scalp. Bending forward, she wrapped the works into a towel turban, letting the warmth of her head seal in the oils and botanicals. The cotton wrap cushioned her head as she lay back, ready for the tub level to rise so she could push the start button and bubble away her problems. For a few minutes, at least.

Thunk! Thunk! Thunk!

"Are you going to be in there all day?" Victoria hollered.

"No, just shaving my legs," Grace lied. She ran her hand up her calf to her thigh, feeling the smoothness she had insured the day before. Had it only been twelve hours since she had primped, shaved, and oiled her body to perfection for her 'first time'? And less than six hours since she had kissed Dusty goodbye, the two of them talking about their 'next time' and a shared forever?

"I want you downstairs and dressed in ten minutes. We have work to do," Victoria said, then smacked the door again to punctuate her command.

"Yes, Mother," Grace replied dispassionately, then pushed the Jacuzzi pump button, obliterating the chance of hearing anything else from her ruthless parent. She looked at the digital clock on the sink counter, noting the time. "I won't be late."

Sinking down to her towel-wrapped hair, Grace let the water jets work their magic on her tense muscles. "Minute by minute," she reminded herself, inhaling deeply, recalling the scent of her lover's musky chest, the feel of two of his five chest hairs as they tickled her nose. Her eyes closed for a moment, then popped open to see the time.

"Crap!" She scooted down in the tub, ran her fingers through her hair to work out as much conditioner as she could in ten seconds, then stood up, hastily drying as much of her hair and body as she could before grabbing the dressing gown hanging on the hook. *Thirty seconds left!*

She rushed downstairs and slowed two steps before the kitchen door, catching her breath and reminding herself to keep her remarks to herself.

“Is that how you plan on finding a husband?” Victoria sneered, eyeing Grace head to flip-flop shod toes, then taking another drag off her cigarette.

“You said dressed and I am. I didn’t know it was for an interview. If you’d like, I can go back and change.”

Victoria flicked invisible ash from the end of her cigarette into the marble ashtray, then picked up her *demitasse* cup of coffee, pinkie extended. “No. Don’t bother. This is just the first step. We need to peruse these to find one who looks more or less like your little boy toy. I really can’t remember much about him other than he was fair-skinned and as lanky as a two-by-four clothesline. His build had promise with those broad shoulders, but as the son of a groundskeeper, he may as well have been a twenty-year-old garden rake.

Keep quiet. Don’t comment. Get through this conversation. She’ll wear out eventually. Or she’ll find something else to keep her occupied. Remember, minute by minute.

Picking up the photo album at her elbow, Victoria opened it to the tab marked ‘B.’ “If you had been accepted – or your father and I had purchased your acceptance – into a top tier college, the ‘A’ list men would have been an option. Not as many to choose from as the ‘B’ list, but their pedigree and net worth are so much more desirable.”

Grace couldn’t help it. She hissed the harsh words even before they had formed them in her head. “Is that all love and marriage are to you?”

Undaunted by the context but surprised that Grace had lost her cool so soon after her first ‘attitude adjustment,’ Victoria decided to let this one slide. Her daughter had, after all, been sleep deprived and was still in shock at her new status in life as an adult. “Marriage is a social arrangement; a legal business contract. Love is something that comes and goes; a fondness for a cute puppy that quickly grows into frustration with an uncontrollable, mangy cur. Men are nothing but skirt-chasing, turd-dropping burdens who ruin your holidays.”

“Oh, so that’s what this is about; you’re mad at Daddy?”

In a flash, Victoria was on her feet, her diamond-ringed fist clenching Grace’s throat. “You know, it really isn’t too late for more rape injuries to be inflicted. I have a wine bottle or two that could do some real damage.”

Just as quickly as she had grabbed her, Victoria released her, dropping her hand to her side, settling back into the chair at the table as if nothing had happened, scanning the newspaper clippings of the men on the first page of the ‘B’ candidates.

Grace was stunned by the sudden assault, the physical result of choking even worse than the emotional distress. She tried to relax her throat muscles, doing everything she could not to puke and humiliate herself further. *I gotta get out of here!*

“Oh, and don’t even think about leaving,” Victoria said as if reading her thoughts. “Remember, I know your little boy toy’s daddy. It wouldn’t take much to ruin both of them with the accusation of a father and son rape. After all, some men might like that kind of thing. You know, sharing a woman. Or a girl. After all, you are only seventeen,” she said, then added a sinister smirk.

Don’t talk. She’s baiting you. You already had this conversation. She wants you to argue. Facts mean nothing. She can manipulate anything.

“Ah, obedient silence,” Victoria said. “I like that. Keep it up and we’ll get along just fine. Now, come sit next to Mother and point out which ones you think would work for you. Mind the notes in the margin: net worth, location, and height. We’ll have to read through the text to see how many siblings. Those who don’t have any at all are in the ‘C’ list. Let’s hope we don’t have to sink that far.”

I’ve already sunk that far…

“How about this one?” Victoria asked.

Grace turned the binder around and glanced at the society page photo of a man who seemed to be similar in looks to Dusty. The notes said, ‘Stockbroker, two brothers, one possibly gay, the other an architect.

"Sure. Why not?" Grace said, then sunk back in the chair and looked at the wine chiller, stocked with bottles for the week's meals. *You may become my next best friend.*

Chapter 3
Setting the Bait

Victoria picked up her black leather-bound monthly planner, checked the annual calendar on the back page for reference, then switched back and forth to the current month, comparing notes. "Well, it looks like we're in luck. You'll have to skip a couple of days of school, but I think we can make it. I'll just say I forgot to bring our invitations."

"Make it to what?" Grace asked, reaching for one of the fresh-baked muffins.

Victoria smacked her hand. "None of that until we find your Mister Right. If you're on the skinny side, a man will feel sorry for you and want to take you under his wing and fatten you up."

"Like a calf? Lucky me."

Victoria's jaw clenched and her hand flew up, ready to instill an obedience adjustment when she heard the housekeeper shuffling toward the breakfast nook. Her fingers fluttered down, settling harmlessly to the side of her head, pushing some of her perfectly coifed hair behind her ear, her attention back to her social events scheduler.

The housekeeper looked around, sensing the tension. "What's the matter, Missy?" she asked, and briefly set her hand on Grace's shoulder to reassure her. She patted it twice, then brought the platter of muffins closer, setting a clean plate in front of the young woman she had looked after for over a decade. "I baked these just for you this morning. I know how much you love them." She paused and looked around at the sparsely set table. "Oh, that's right. You like them with lots of butter. Here, I'll get some out of the pantry for you."

"Oh, don't bother, Sally," Grace said. "I'm not ready for breakfast yet. Thanks anyhow. I'm sure they'll be just as great at lunch."

"Ooh, that does sound good. Maybe with a bit of cream cheese and preserves? Makes me hungry all over again and I already ate two of them."

"Good morning, everyone," Hal said brightly, swatting Sally's ample rear end playfully with the rolled-up newspaper. "The Times isn't good for much else," he said to her, then set the paper on the table. "You're not going to call sexual harassment on me, are you?" he whispered in her ear.

"Not as long as you keep giving me those big Christmas bonuses, I won't," she said, grabbing a plate for him. "Care to join your family?"

Hal glanced at Victoria and a chill shot up his spine. She was tenser than usual, her bony shoulders pulled further back, chin higher in the air. She was wearing her iron maiden attitude, ready for battle with whoever was nearby.

Then he noticed Grace. She was biting her bottom lip, blinking back tears, avoiding looking up at him. He'd seen that look before but not since her Sweet Sixteen party. Victoria had made her miserable, embarrassed her in front of all her friends, then acted like Grace was overreacting when her friends decided they'd better leave early. Apparently, something had just happened between the two. He swallowed hard and looked at Sally to see if she had noticed.

The robust housekeeper and cook had taken two mini bran muffins and added them to a plate of fresh orange slices. "I made some small ones so I wouldn't feel too bad if I ate four of them. Try these! I added dried cherries instead of raisins to this batch. It really kicked them up a notch."

Grace looked over at her former nanny and a genuine smile emerged. Sally looked back at Hal and gave him one of her all-knowing winks. *That woman won't bedevil your daughter while both of us are here.*

With the wink, Hal scooted back and relaxed into the chair he'd been sitting on the edge of. Sally was a decent cook, a passable housekeeper, but also the most nurturing woman he'd ever encountered. He wasn't in love with her but was eternally grateful that she was in his life. Or at least, in Grace's life.

"So, I was thinking of taking Grace to the regatta next week," Victoria said, her voice more assertive than usual.

"I don't think that's a good idea," Hal said. He poured a cup of coffee, knowing she'd have a retort. As soon as she cleared her voice to speak, he continued his thought, intentionally talking over her. "It's her last week of school before graduation. It's one of the most socially active times of her high school experience. This is her last chance to spend time with the friends she grew up with before she takes off to college. Bryn Mawr is so lucky to get you."

"What?" Grace squealed, popping up out of her chair and her doldrums.

"Yup, they're lucky to get you. You see, since my mother went there, you're a legacy. One generation removed, but that was close enough when I offered an endowment." Hal looked away, paused, then caught his daughter's eye. "Nah. Just messing with you…"

Her glee popped like a soap bubble, Grace sat back in the cushioned kitchen chair, ready to set her chin on her knuckles.

"Whoa! Wait!" he said, rushing over to hold her close, clutching her in a half-hug. "I wasn't joking about being accepted at Bryn Mawr; just the endowment part."

He pulled away and looked at her. He saw her tears fall then felt them reappear on his face. "You got in on your grades and extracurricular activities. The acceptance letter was mailed months ago, but for some reason, it never got here. I called about it, wanted to know if they had made their determinations and if so, did they possibly have some wiggle room for the daughter of a son of a daughter of Bryn Mawr. They were surprised by the call. They figured you had accepted somewhere else."

Hal shot a glare at Victoria but remained mute. He didn't need to let everyone know that the college told him they had received a letter of declination signed by Grace. By his daughter's ecstatic reaction on hearing she was accepted, he knew someone in the house had drafted a fake response and forged the signature. One hundred to one it wasn't Sally or anyone else not married to him.

Getting Grace out of the house and away from her toxic mother couldn't come soon enough. His face reddened as he choked down his frustration. His wife's jealousy of her own daughter was bad enough, but she had taken it a giant step beyond that. Ever since he could remember, she had been presenting Grace with a skewed outlook on life. She insisted that women of their social status should consider the importance of improving, or at least maintaining, the breeding line. Suggestions were constantly being dropped to Grace that she needed to enhance her face and figure with surgeries and silicone to ensure she was attractive to a suitable mate. A good marriage was the only way she would be able to afford a comfortable existence and a place for dear mommy if and when said mommy was kicked to the curb.

Hal knew that it was only a matter of time before Victoria screwed up and he caught her having an affair. He needed to catch her literally with her pants down if not in the act itself. If he even hinted at a separation or divorce, she'd bleed him beyond death, leaving him as empty as a desiccated corpse without even a beggar's cup for Grace. He didn't have any valid grounds against her. Yet. As soon as she was caught being unfaithful or deceitful or any of those other 'fuls' with a negative connotation, he'd have her in divorce court so fast, her two-faced head would spin off her skinny neck. He blessed his mother daily for insisting on an ironclad prenuptial. It was the only thing that kept him sane. Hope. Hope for him and his daughter.

"No," Victoria said pointedly, then lit another cigarette.

Hal coughed at the smoke and pushed the battery-powered smoke eater towards her. "If you don't mind," he said. *And even if you do...*

"No, what?" Grace asked, peering hopefully at her mother.

"No, you won't be attending the last few days of school. We had an agreement, remember?"

"What's all this about?" Hal asked, standing close to his

daughter, hand on her shoulder in reassurance.

Victoria's scowl deepened as she glared at Grace. When Grace didn't flinch, she picked up a wine bottle and ran her hand up and down the neck of it. "I think we should have *coq au vin* tonight, don't you, Sally?" she asked. "I'd like the bottle when you're done with it…"

Grace's eyes widened in shock. *You'd rape your own daughter with a wine bottle just to get your own way? And ruin the lives of two others at the same time, both of them innocent?*

Victoria smirked and shook her head at Grace. *You can't win. You play my game and let me win; or you fight me and you, your boyfriend, and his lawn-cutting daddy all lose. Which one?*

Grace looked up at her father, letting a shadow of disappointment show. "Mother and I were talking about this earlier," she said truthfully, knowing she was a lousy liar. "She made some very strong points for taking off before school was out. I'm sure my friends will have a good time without me." *Even if I'm going to be setting myself up for a miserable existence, seeking out whatever husband she decides is right for me. Oh, for an early death!*

***

"Not bad," Victoria said as she looked over the linen-covered tables laden with silver chafing dishes of hot meats and sauces, and cut-crystal platters of fresh fruits, canapes, and intricately carved and formed vegetables. "Just make sure you pick up something quick to chew and swallow that won't stick in your teeth or stain them. Better yet, just grab some celery to play with. Give them a little preview of how sweet your long fingers will look, running up and down…"

"Mother!" Grace hissed. She cleared her throat, nodding to a worried man who looked to be the butler or someone else in charge of keeping order. She quickly got her embarrassment under control and asked, "You did get the invitation situation cleared up, I hope." *Oh, Lord, I hope you didn't get it cleared up. If they throw us out, we'll be ruined. Even F-list men won't want me. I'll be free again!*

"Silas!" Victoria gushed, her hand out, ready to paw the arm of the man in charge of checking invitations. "I didn't know you worked in this neighborhood. Nice digs," she added, nodding to the elaborate ice sculptures on the tables, then the young men rushing back and forth with trays of champagne flutes.

"I'm doing well, thank you for asking," Silas said guilelessly, then looked aside, as if he wished she hadn't spotted him.

"Oh, and this is my daughter, Grace. Say hello to Silas, dear," she prompted. Her hand lay on Grace's forearm, fingers clutching gently, reminding her to play her part.

Grace looked to make sure her mother was turned away, watching for available suitors, before she said, "Hello, Silas," then mouthed the word, 'dear.'

Silas's mouth twitched in a grin as she playfully repeated what her mother had told her to, then quickly returned to somber when he saw Victoria look back at them. "It's a pleasure," he said. He turned to Victoria and added, "If there's anything I can do for you, Mrs. Stillwater, please don't hesitate to ask."

"Well, now that you mention it, Silas," she said, her hands leaving Grace and settling on his upper arm. "We would love an introduction to one, or all, of the Armstrong brothers. You see, it doesn't really make a difference which one we meet *first*," Victoria said. "I hear they're all such interesting men."

Silas flashed his phony smile, acknowledging the truth of what she had just said, but hiding his true feelings from her. His stomach knotted at being near this social lamprey who was obviously siccing her disinterested daughter on whichever of the rich brothers took a fancy to her.

The gentleman's gentleman had first encountered Victoria Stillwater years ago when he was working for another family and she was still a newlywed. She was slobbering drunk at the time, and he had only been employed by the banker and his family for a week when she hit on him. She rubbed her bony fanny up against him, then turned and grabbed him in the crotch when she thought no one was looking. He covered up the shock of her fumbled clutch, pretending he had a sudden gut pain, but his boss had seen the whole episode. The only good that had come out of her botched flirt was his employer had seen that he was capable of discretion under pressure.

He stayed with the banker until he died, enjoying a comfortable relationship with the confirmed bachelor. In appreciation, the old man left him his huge house and a very comfortable inheritance.

Silas no longer *had* to work but still very much enjoyed the people watching – the social sambas and tangos – that blossomed at galas and parties. He let it be known to local families that he would be available for big events where a cool head and discerning eye were needed – situations like tonight where multiple party-crashers had already dropped in. Some of the revelers were looking for introductions, others to pinch a silver salver or two, a few just wanting free food and drink. Discretion in ejecting wayward sorts was a top priority; bad publicity and the need for law enforcement was to be avoided.

He looked up, presumably searching for one of the young Armstrong men, but really trying to read the beautiful young girl with dark blonde hair. She couldn't be more than a recent high school graduate, a gentle soul who appeared to have no interest in her mother's hunt for a husband for her. The sadness behind the young girl's eyes couldn't be hidden by the expert application of makeup or the feigned smile that was fading as the moments passed.

Yes, his gut impression was right. It was the mother who was on the prowl, seeking a mate for her pup. It was obvious to him that the humbled lass had her sights set on someone who was not in this thoroughbred stable. More than likely, she had chosen an open range mustang and Mom had shotgunned him out of the territory, scared him away with emasculating threats.

"Oh, isn't that one of the sons?" Victoria exclaimed, grabbing Silas's arm, bringing him out of his introspection. She realized what she had done, glad that she had only nodded in Alex's direction and not pointed. "Isn't that Armando?" she asked.

"No, ma'am," Silas said, enunciating the generic salutation, refusing to call her by name. "That is Alexander, although I don't think anyone ever calls him by his full name. I suggest Alex for addressing him."

"Oh, yes," Victoria agreed. "Al is such a common name. It sounds like the name of a plumber or car mechanic, not an architect."

Silas glanced over at the young woman. She was suppressing a grin at her mother's obvious prejudice when it came to names, snapping back to primness when her mother turned her way.

"It looks like he's ready for a fresh drink," Silas said. "Let me see if he's available."

As soon as her social coordinator was out of earshot, Victoria clutched Grace's arm, her fingers digging into the bare flesh. Grace flinched and her mother relaxed her grip, hoping she hadn't inadvertently left a mark. "Remember to let him do the talking. It's fine to give him prompts. Ask him about his latest project, where he likes to vacation, anything positive." She looked up and saw Silas speaking with him, then glancing her way. "Smile, Grace. Show him your perfect teeth, but don't open your mouth too wide. I don't want you to appear too eager."

Grace smiled at the irony. *Eager? I'm the opposite of eager.* Her slight smile widened as she noticed the eye roll of the party manager. *Looks like Silas has us pegged. I may be missing the parties with my friends, but if Mother gets her comeuppance at this gala, it will be worth it.*

Perfectly at peace for the first time since her mother had 'caught and broke' her, Grace was radiant in her momentary serenity as the two men approached. She briefly caught the scent of her mother's perfume, her body's nervous sweat setting off the high-dollar aroma. *Better her than me. She's a nervous wreck! And I am so enjoying her discomfort...*

"Mrs. Victoria Stillwater," Silas said, positioning himself

between the two parties. "May I introduce the first son of our host. This is Alexander Armstrong," winking at the man when he used the full version of his first name.

"Alex," he said, winking back, then accepted the proffered hand. He reached to shake it, then realized Victoria was holding it up for him to kiss. He stifled his chuckle at the formality and brushed his lips across her cold knuckles. He stood up and looked at the young woman beside her. "And you are?"

"I'm sorry," Silas said. "I didn't get your name, Miss."

"I'm Grace Elizabeth Stillwater, but Grace or 'Hey, you!' will get my attention," she said, making sure she didn't laugh out loud at her own joke.

"Well, then, Grace it is," Alex said, now totally intrigued with the good-looking party crasher. "Silas, why don't you show Mrs. Stillwater to the more comfortable seating inside. I think Grace and I would like to take a walk. You would like to see the stables, wouldn't you?"

"You have horses?" Grace asked, then playfully smacked her forehead. "Let's hope so. I don't think you have stables for camels or ostriches…or do you?"

Alex put his arm across her shoulder. "Where have you been all my life?" he asked, then looked back to make sure they wouldn't be followed.

Silas's hand was on Victoria's elbow, urging her toward the pavilion. "Let's leave them alone, shall we?"

Victoria took a step to follow the young couple, then halted. She'd have to trust Grace not to blow her first chance at bedding the billionaire's son. Then again, there were still two more brothers. It would serve the brat right if she did choose the wrong one the first time.

Chapter 4
Alex the Architect

"I don't think I've ever seen you before at one of these events," Alex said to Grace, snagging a glass of champagne from the server's tray as he passed. He handed it to her and smiled.

She accepted it reluctantly, holding it by the stem, pinkie extended like it might bite her if she approached it wrong. "I'm not sure about the law in Massachusetts, but I'm only eighteen. Actually, I don't think I'm old enough to drink in any state," she said and handed the flute back to the shocked server.

Alex whispered in her ear. "No one's carding tonight. If you'd like one, go ahead. If not, let me know, and I'll have Sam bring you whatever your heart desires."

Grace giggled. "Does he have access to root beer?"

"With or without ice cream?"

An abbreviated chuckle escaped, then she took a deep breath, using the moment to figure out what she should do. "Surprise me. Mother would have a fit if she saw me eating or drinking sweets. She already thinks I'm too fat."

Alex eyed her up and down, adding an exaggerated frown of disapproval. "I'd say fewer bagels in the morning might take care of that belly roll. Oh, and skipping the cream cheese might help erase one or two of those extra chins."

"You're hilarious," Grace said. "And here I thought I was going to be miserable tonight."

"Hey, the night's still young." He looked over at his father and shook his head.

"Someone you know?" Grace asked, noticing his sudden change in demeanor.

"Yup. All my life."

Grace moved over to his other side and noticed her mother fawning over the man Alex had been eyeing. He was tall and handsome; except for the silver hair, an older version of the man beside her. "Yup. Parents. What are you going to do with 'em? You can't claim they're not yours with DNA tests getting more and more accurate, and they refuse to run away from home."

"Yeah," Alex replied in the same dry tone. "And no matter how much you scream or pout or try to distract them, they keep trying to live your life for you."

"Amen to that!" Grace said, then grabbed Alex's glass of champagne and chugged the contents.

"I thought you were too young to drink."

"I am. But I'm not too young to have my mother totally ruin my life." She saw her dilemma waving at her and returned her gesture with the empty glass. "And yours?"

"Don't have one. Mom died a long time ago," Alex said. He took the champagne flute from her. "And I may not be *your* parent, but I do think you're too young to drink. Sorry, I don't mean to be bossing you around or telling you what to do, but I'd protect a stranger the same way if she was walking in front of a truck."

"Yup. That's my mother. A highjacked firetruck, rushing in to take over someone's situation with loud noises and flashing bling. Always trying to alter the course of people's lives whether it's any of her business or not."

"Wow! You're pretty sharp. I take it she's already trying to commandeer your life?"

"Already? Try the word still. My father and nanny did as much as they could to insulate me from her, but once I turned eighteen, my nanny was out the door. Or she would have been if my father hadn't decided that we needed a full-time housekeeper and cook. She was already doing those jobs, too, but Mother wanted my warm-blooded comforter and confidant gone. Dad insisted she stay but did give in a little. She's only part-time now. That leaves way too many hours in the day that I'm vulnerable."

"What about your father? Are your parents still married? I mean, it'd be a miracle if they were."

"Yes, they're still married. No, it's not a miracle. It's called an ironclad pre-nuptial agreement. I think my father wishes he'd never had it drafted that way. It was to protect him from the poor money-grabber who was carrying his child. Me. Yes, I have plenty of guilt with that one. He'd have his freedom now except they're supposed to be active in each other's lives, blah, blah, blah. I guess he thought he loved her at some point. I've seen what it really was with other couples since, though. He didn't love her; he loved the child she was carrying. Yup. Still me. I don't know if they've even had sex in the last however many years. She tenses up when he gets near, even though he's not the least bit attentive to her."

"Maybe with some therapy…"

"No way, José," Grace said, laughing out loud. She looked over at her mother and noticed she had moved to the other side of their host, making sure she could observe the young couple in their first encounter even if she couldn't supervise or direct them. "She says therapy is for losers; that there isn't a problem that can't be solved with a few bottles of wine and a gold card. I'd tell you more, but this is a party and we're supposed to be having fun. Or celebrating something. I'm not sure which."

"Come on, Grace," Alex said, his arm around her shoulder. "Let's get some real food into that cute little belly of yours. Alcohol on an empty stomach is just inviting trouble."

Rather than move away from the man she had just met, Grace leaned into him, appreciating the warmth and solidness of his body, a reminder that there was someone who could literally stand between her and her abusive mother. "I assume you know the way?" she asked whimsically.

"If I didn't, I'd still find sustenance for you. You're as skinny as a maverick separated from the herd."

Thunk!

His soft-spoken comment was a reminder of her mother's advice to be thin to get a man's attention – to entice him to want to take care of little girl lost. Alex had certainly meant nothing by it, but it still made her feel as if her heart was a six-pound stone that had been dropped into a puddle of mud – dirty and worthless.

Grace was in a daze of disappointment as her broad-shouldered champion led her through the maze of gala attendees. Most of the chatter among the couples and small groups was about the upcoming regatta. Evidently, Robert Van der Cleft's wife was to make an appearance. Bets were being taken as to whether she'd be as stunning as she had been in the past. The woman was due to have a baby by Christmas. She insisted that regaining her figure would be 'no big deal;' that women who didn't take care of themselves were just lazy.

"I saw Zelda Van der Cleft last week," Alex said, holding his hands out to indicate a big belly. "I don't know much about pregnancies and babies, but if she can shrink down to a bikini body two months after she delivers, she deserves her husband's money."

"What's a shapely figure have to do with anything?" Grace asked, accepting the plate from the caterer with a nod and a quick smile. "Do you think a woman has to be built like a brick shithouse to be worthy of her husband's money…or his affections?"

"No, no, that's not what I meant. Oh, crap," Alex said, looking into the crowd, trying to find a reason to leave the uncomfortable conversation. "Hey, I see someone I have to speak with," he lied. "Would you excuse me?"

"Of course. I don't have any claim on you. It's your party. I'm just the teenager whose mother decided…" She blanched at her near confession, turned away, and swallowed her groan.

Certainly, he already knew or suspected that her mother had brought her to the party of rich single men to find a husband. What did he care about her and her feelings as long as he had a good time? She was just a warm garage he hoped to park his hot rod in before the night was over. If she wasn't available, there were plenty of other skinny, painted females around.

"What happened to him?"

Grace tensed at her mother's hissed question, the canapes and curled carrot sticks slipping off her plate onto the grass. She quietly counted to five, then answered, "He had to speak with someone. Why?"

"What? Why?" Victoria sputtered. She looked around to make sure they didn't have an audience, then whispered harshly through a fake smile, "You're here to make a good impression on at least two if not all three of the brothers. You haven't been here twenty minutes and you've already scared him off!"

"Au, contraire, Mama." Grace stepped back to the ornate expanse of *hors d'oeuvres,* picked out a couple of crab puffs and at the same time, kicked her spilled food under the table. "He and I were connecting very well before he spotted an important business associate. You don't want him to lose his wealth by spending all his time with the new love of his life, do you?" Grace nodded to Alex who was speaking with an elderly gentleman. She gave a perfect Miss America wave to him, her smile as inviting as an engraved invitation.

Alex paused his conversation with his father's chauffeur when he saw Grace waving at him. He waved back. *It looks like she needs to be saved from Mother Imperator. Rescue the damsel and I still might get lucky after all.*

"Excuse me, Gregory," Alex said, accepting the fob with two keys. "This should do for tonight. Thanks for letting me in. I know it's supposed to be reserved for special occasions for Dad, but tonight is special for me. Or I hope it is."

Gregory followed Alex's gaze. The innocent standing beside Victoria Stillwater must be her daughter. He hadn't seen her since she was in grade school. If she was who Alex was planning to devour, he'd better make sure the young man spoke with his father first. There was more at stake than just a little romp in the rose garden.

"By the way," Gregory said, his hand covering Alex's key-clutching fist. "I believe your father wanted to speak with you on a very important matter before you get carried away. Make sure you let him know you'll be using the garden house, too. Oh, and he'll be interested to know that you've made the acquaintance of Hal Stillwater's daughter. Those two go way back. I'm sure he'll be thrilled at the prospect of a family alliance."

Alex's hand went limp at the hint of what was in store if he dallied with this new infatuation. Now he knew why Gregory had made the odd gesture of holding onto him. He would have dropped the keys like they were molten metal if he had known. "Why?"

"Does it make a difference if you're already attracted to her? She's a wonderful young lady. Her mother, not so much. Your father will let you know more. I do believe he's at the boathouse now."

"I smell a skunk," Alex said, his lips pursed in frustration.

"No, not a skunk," Gregory said. "That's Chuck. He's down the way, smoking with a few of the guests."

"Let's hope Dad doesn't have much to say. If I'm more than a few minutes, would you make sure Grace knows I won't be long?"

Gregory smiled devilishly. "I think I'll go over there now and make your excuse. I'd love to trade jabs with Victoria. I have no attraction to that woman at all, but it would almost be worth having an affair with her just to get it on tape. Having proof like that is the only way Hal would be able to divorce her."

"What are you talking about, Gregory? Have you been smoking with Chuck and the boys? Your brain-mouth filter seems to be missing."

"As a matter of fact, I am slightly stoned. Of course, if I weren't, I wouldn't be admitting it. Nevertheless, talk to your father. You'll see why tonight my restraints are made of tissue, not leather or steel."

"Thanks for the warning." Alex reached up and patted Gregory on the shoulder with his free hand, letting the long-time chauffeur and family friend know that he'd regained his composure. "And see if you can insulate Grace from that monster mother of hers. I hate to say it, but that skinny Medusa is the number one reason I wouldn't want to get serious about Grace. She gives me the shivers."

“You and me both.”

It didn’t take long for Alex to find his father. Evidently, he had been watching for him. As soon as the son was over the rise and in view of the boathouse, ‘Papa Doc’ Armstrong was out from the shadows of the painted wood enclosure and out in the open.

“How’s my favorite eldest son tonight?” his father asked brightly.

“I’m fine. Gregory said you wanted to talk to me. He also said to make sure to tell you that I’ve taken a shine to Hal Stillwater’s daughter. She and I might be spending more time together,” Alex said, then brought the cabin’s keys up and jingled them.

“Hal Stillwater?” Papa Doc asked with a frown, then a smile rose as he remembered who he was. “Oh, I so would appreciate you getting along with his daughter. Her name’s Faith, isn’t it?”

“Close. It’s Grace. She’s here with her mother tonight. I have the sneaking suspicion that they crashed the party. At least, that’s what I read in Silas’s face.”

“Yes, that man has a way of hiding his true feelings but letting what he wants to say be read with a twitch or sneer or lift of an eyebrow.”

“So, Dad, what’s going on? Gregory said you wanted to speak with me about something.”

His father sighed and shook his head, the harbinger of bad news. “Looks like the big C might be back. I’m okay for right now, but I might need your help in making some transitions. I don’t trust Ben farther than I can shove him, and Chuck has no interest in the business. In other words, the funds ain’t what they used to be so don’t go buying any new houses or Picassos.”

“Dad, I haven’t used your money for anything since I got the firm going. My architectural designs are in high demand. I didn’t expect to be this successful for years. And if I’m reading you right, you’re saying that all those high risk-great rewards stocks my sweet brother Ben told you to buy were not only duds, they were devastating.”

"It wouldn't be so bad, but after the first round went south, he tried to get me to make it up with another investment. I finally had to say no when he tried to salvage it with a third swing. 'Three strikes and I'll be out,' I told him. I finally had to walk away. Anyhow, it can be repaired. If I can entice Stillwater to joint venture with me, we'll both be sitting pretty. There was some bad blood between us a few years back. And by that, I mean nearly twenty years ago. It had to do with that evil woman he wound up marrying." Papa Doc shuddered as he recalled her seducing him right after her honeymoon. "How he could live with that evil witch is beyond me."

"I'm in agreement there, even if I've never met him. You might want to stay here for a while. Sweet Grace is up there with her now. You don't want to bump into her."

"Thanks for the warning. Be nice to Grace. If you two spark up a romance, be polite. And careful. Not that I wouldn't want a grandchild or two, but if our two families are going to be working together, I don't want there to be animosity over a soured affair."

"Our family businesses working together," Alex corrected. "And I'm always gentle in my goodbyes. I learned from the master." He reached over and gave his father a quick hug. "And Master, please stop acting on Ben's crazy schemes. You can listen to him; just don't sign anything or give him money. Remind him that you started with nothing and have the world." He spread his hands out, indicating the vast properties. "He, on the other hand, started out with millions and is winding up with nothing."

"Well, just don't go rubbing it in. He already has short bald-man syndrome. He doesn't need any more insecurities. Now, go put a smile on that young woman's face. And see if you can get one of those *paparazzi* to get a picture of the two of you for the tabloids. That will definitely work in our favor."

"No problem there. I'm sure Old Mother Stillwater has already nudged them in that direction. Plus, all I'd have to do is look like I'm trying to avoid them, and they'll be on me like gnats on a jelly donut. I'll tell you all about it at lunch tomorrow. Or not, depending on how the evening goes."

"Go! No details required," Papa Doc said. *Just don't do anything that would piss off her father.*

Alex half-walked, half-sprinted up the hill, his pace quickening when he saw Grace turn to watch him approach.

"I thought you'd ditched me," she said, her eyes squinted in playful admonishment.

"I couldn't get back here fast enough," Alex said, glad to see that Mother had left the immediate area. "One important conversation led to another. By the way, the last one was with my father. He remembers you from long ago. Did we ever meet?"

"Not that I recall," Grace answered. "I don't think I've ever met any of my father's friends or their families. All social events are coordinated by Mother. Maybe she knows your father."

"Shush," Alex said, then winked. "Let's not talk about parents tonight, shall we? How about a walk. I have something special I'd like to show you."

"If you mean ditch my mother, I'm all in, even if it's just to watch windmills turn."

"Not quite as exciting," Alex said drolly, then kissed the side of her hair. "Sorry, I probably shouldn't have done that. Must be the champagne."

"I'd like to think at least a little bit of it was me."

"All of it was you. The alcohol removed the last little bit of inhibition. Come on, let's split. If your mother tries to give you any flack, just tell her the host wanted you to mingle. Or to show you off, depending on how she feels about me."

Grace opened her mouth to continue the playful banter, then shut it again and silently considered what to say. She decided it was best to remain mysterious; to squeeze his arm playfully and remain mum. She'd let him lead. Anything was better than going back to Mother.

Ah, smart woman. Not too gabby. She knows it's better to be coy and mysterious than chatty and annoying. Alex looked around for the ever-present society photographers. Drat! The one time he wanted them in his face, they were taking a bathroom break. Or with the marijuana smokers.

"Let's walk this way," Alex suggested, rerouting them to the garden house via the shrubbery maze where the pot party was.

A hundred yards into their trek, Grace couldn't help but ask, her nose twitching, "Are there skunks around here?"

"Are you kidding? This is a high society party. There are dozens of skunks!" Alex laughed at his own joke, glad that she was chuckling, too. And then he saw them: two of the most ambitious *paparazzi* on the eastern seaboard. He looked over and caught Jimmy's eye and winked. *Got one for you. It's okay to follow.*

Jimmy nudged his partner, causing the man to quickly drop the joint and step on it, hiding his evidence. "Huh? Oh, yeah. Good find. They're going to eat this one up," he whispered. "She's a hottie. Young, too. Do you know who she is?"

"Not a clue," Jimmy answered. "I'll let Jaylene figure that one out. She knows everyone and their kids. Let's just hope for his sake that's she's legal. Looks like he's taking her up to the garden house."

"Yup," the assistant whispered. "The infamous house of deflowering."

Jimmy glared at him and he rephrased the comment. "Okay, so most of the gals who go up there aren't innocent, but quite a few petals have been pushed and poked within those four walls."

"Yeah," Jimmy chuckled, "what I wouldn't give to have a spy camera in there. We'd never have to chase society snobs and actors again."

Jimmy started following the couple, knowing his backup cameraman was running ahead, snapping photos of their approach to the hideaway. *And if I can sneak in after their tryst, odds are that there's already a hidden video camera. All I have to do is snag the tape. I don't even have to sell it to the highest bidder. I'll just let it be known that I have it and get a monthly blackmail check from the family!*

"And here's one of the most beautiful gardens on the eastern seaboard," Alex said, opening the gate of the white picket fence.

"How beautiful!" Grace said. "Is this where you stay or is this just for *special* occasions?" she asked, winking at him.

Alex moved closer, changing the atmosphere of their casual friendship with his nearness, their skin-to-skin contact hopefully leading them into the lover zone. "I think you still have a little champagne in your system," he cooed into her hair, nuzzling her ear, making sure there wasn't a tree or building in the way of the photographer's lens.

"Very little," Grace said softly and turned to look at him in the soft light afforded by the garden's floodlamp. "And I think I could get used to the taste. Do you happen to have more inside?"

"Ooh, I like that," Alex said. He gently touched her elbow again, leading her to the front porch. He pushed in the access code and opened the door. Looking back into nothingness, he shook his head briefly, letting Jimmy know the photoshoot was over. The rest of the evening was just for him and his latest lady love.

"Are you ready for what waits inside?" he asked.

Grace's fake smile fell as fear covered her in a nervous sweat. It hadn't been too bad – the teasing had actually been kind of fun – but now it was pay-up time. Could she be intimate with someone other than Dusty? Her blank features darkened as she considered her options. Or her single option. It was either spread her legs for the handsome and charming man or go home with Mother. Try to find as many likable aspects of the billionaire's son or listen to her abusive parent chastise her for being a failure. Or worse: feel her mother's blows. Yes, bring on the liquor. Hopefully, it would make it all tolerable. At least Mother wasn't trying to hook her up with some ancient rich widower.

***

"Are you sure she knew where I was?" Grace asked, pulling the sheets up over the bottom of her face to contain her morning breath.

"Positive," Alex said. "I texted Silas and asked him to tell your mother that you and I had made plans for the rest of the evening."

"What kind of plans did you say?"

"I didn't. I left that up to him. He's pretty creative. He reads people well. He'd be able to tell if she needed to hear that I was flying you up to New York City to watch the opening of a highly acclaimed off-Broadway show or take you out for a midnight sail. Or anything else."

"So, this is a usual party night for you? Find a sweet young thing and have your way with her?"

"No," Alex said, then chuckled. "Now, come on. We're both adults. Or at least you did tell me you were eighteen. That means that legally you're an adult, even if you don't have a lot of life experience under your belt." He looked over at her clothes laid over the chair beside the bed. "Or lack of belt. No, most of the women who come up here are older and more experienced. I try to stay away from anyone who is marriageable if that even is a word."

"I believe it is," Grace said dryly, remembering that she still had to bed at least one more of the brothers. "Does that mean the women you usually 'entertain' are already married?"

"I should be ashamed to admit it, but I'm not. Yes, married women are very good lovers. They know what they're doing. Or rather, they are more adventurous. From what they tell me, once they've married, their love life goes downhill. It's the same three-minute special for sex, once or twice a month. Maybe more often if she has an extensive library of porn videos and exotic apparel and knows how to put on a show."

"Ew! Really? You'd think that being in love with your mate would be enough," Grace said. The words echoed in her head as she realized where she was and with whom. She had just played the whore. She was no better than the horny man in front of her who took advantage of cheating wives by giving them an afternoon or evening of carnal kicks. There hadn't been any love involved in what she had done last night. It was strictly booze and friction. And frustration.

"Love and marriage don't necessarily go hand in hand," Alex said as casually as if he was telling her how to spell cat. "And I hate to say it, but from where I stand, the love a couple has in the beginning quickly fades after being married. Maybe it never was love but only an infatuation. Then again, it could be it's the commitment itself – feeling trapped with only one sex partner, home, or life goal. Or it could also be that the added responsibility of living up to your mate's expectations sucks the pleasure out of everything."

"Or maybe marriage really is just money and obligations," Grace said, her stomach churning as she thought about her parents.

"Marriage? Money and obligations? How novel," Alex said, then popped up out of bed. "Be back in a flash, then you can take all the time you need in the bathroom. I'll call in for breakfast to be brought over unless you want to go out somewhere. Options are to the big house or anywhere in the world the family jet flies to."

"I'll let you know after freshening up," Grace said, then rolled over and pulled the satin sheets over her head. *How did I wind up here? And how can I get myself out of this mess? What did my mother do to Dusty? Ah, crap! Will he even want me back after this? I might as well be dead!*

True to his word, Alex was out of the bathroom in a short two minutes. He stood above her shield of sheets and realized he felt guilty. *She didn't want this, I know she didn't. I need to help her get her head straight or there could be trouble. The last thing Dad needs is another fiasco. Ben's given him enough to deal with. If I can get her feeling good about herself, at least she won't be a liability.*

"Would you like coffee when you get out of the shower?" he asked. "I have a little espresso machine here. I make a killer cappuccino."

Grace peered up at him, a smile emerging despite her dire

circumstances. His confident voice was a helping hand, offering to help her out of her world of shame. He was a bulwark between her and her mother. She'd be smart to make use of him until she had to face her mother again. She sat up, pulling the sheet over her breasts as she did, then realized he had seen and touched pretty much every bit of flesh and hair on her body the night before. Why hide herself now?

"Coffee? Sure, why not. I feel bad that I don't have any clean clothes to wear. I think my little black dress is a little overkill for breakfast attire," she said, giggling at the thought.

"Don't worry about it." Alex pulled open the hall closet door, exposing a long line of color-coordinated jogging suits. "Just pick your color and length. It's not that I'm a Lothario…"

"Just accommodating," Grace finished. "You know, you really are a nice person. I mean…"

"Nothing you say before your first cup of coffee can be held against you. Take as long as you want to get ready, but sooner is better. It looks like someone forgot to stock the breadbox with fresh pastries." His stomach growled at the word. "Cappuccino with extra cream is going to have to suffice for a while."

She dropped the sheet and stood up. "I didn't bring any makeup, either. Not that I wear much when I do bother with it." She strutted to the closet, suddenly feeling brazen. She swiped aside the neutral-tone clothes and picked out a neon pink suit, checking the length of the pants. "This will do."

"There are a few dozen pairs of new panties in the top drawer there. Sorry. I don't do bras."

Grace stuck out her chest, proud of her perky breasts. "I don't either. I think I'll pass on the panties, too." She saw his drop-jawed stare, taking in her perfect form. "You'd better get started with the coffee, dear. I'm very low maintenance. As long as there's soap and a towel, I'm set."

"Huh? Oh, yeah. It's all in there," he stammered. *Maybe she is worth keeping around...*

Chapter 5
The Morning After

“You’re right. You do make a great cappuccino,” Grace said, sipping the hot contents, leaning forward just in case, cautious of spilling it on her borrowed clothes. Or new clothes. Certainly they weren’t passed back and forth between liaisons!

“Where to for the real food?” she asked, eager to get out of her head and away from all the drama that lived there.

“There’s usually a big morning-after brunch up at the main house. I doubt if anywhere we go would be able to match it. Plus, it’s closer; just a quick jaunt up the hill.”

“How about a slow stroll up the hill; with sunglasses,” Grace suggested. “I think I have my first hangover.”

“Ah, I have a remedy for that. A little crème de menthe will complement the cappuccino plus cool it down. Sorry, I got a little distracted when I was steaming the milk. I would say, ‘Where have you been all my life,’ but besides sounding trite, you were a minor when I was really looking for someone to…to travel with.”

Grace caught his little stutter of infatuation but figured she’d let it slide. After all, neither one of them had eaten yet and a few hours earlier, he had expended a lot of energy with his lovemaking.

Scratch that. With having sex. Despite just having stepped out of the shower, Grace suddenly felt dirty. What she needed now was oblivion. “Will there be mimosas?”

Alex’s unexpectedly bright outlook on life suddenly muddied with the mention of alcohol. Had she always been a lush and hidden it? Or was she just confused and scared, ready to hide behind any substance that masked the real world? A glimmer of hope peeked in as he recalled her mother. “Orange juice, fresh squeezed, with or without the champagne, will be available,” he said. “But this time, let’s make sure you eat something before drinking. It’s just my family around this morning. You can eat all you’d like without anyone *mother*-henning you.”

Relief flooded over Grace with his spot-on words of assurance. She stuck her hand into the crook of his elbow and snuggled close to him, her spiked cappuccino held out at arm's length so neither of them got splashed. "You'd better watch yourself, Alexander Armstrong. I'm beginning to like you."

"Back at ya, Babe," he said and kissed the top of the head. "Come on. Let's go meet more of my family."

***

"Looks like you had company last night," the thirty-something-year-old man with a shaved head and a cocky attitude said.

"Hello, Ben," Alex said, his voice suddenly chilled and formal.

Grace, still holding him close, gently squeezed his arm, letting him know she wouldn't let the cad dressed like he was going to a photoshoot for the local yacht club intimidate her.

Alex sighed with relief at her show of confidence, his feigned smile becoming real with having a friend so near.

"Aren't you going to introduce me to your latest lady love?" Ben sneered, refusing to hold back with his words of intimidation.

"Whoa there, sons," Papa Doc said, stepping between the two, gently elbowing Ben away. "Alex, who is this charming young lady? I don't think I've had the pleasure of being introduced."

"Dad, this is Grace Stillwater. Grace, this is my father, Alexander Benjamin Charles Armstrong, usually called Papa Doc."

"A.B.C. Armstrong," Grace said, accepting his hand. "Don't tell me you have a sister named Deborah Elizabeth Frances Armstrong," she added with a grin.

"Close. Very close. Her first name is Delores, but you got the other names right. Dad said he was going to have a whole alphabet full of children. Mom did her best to shorten the list by giving us all three names."

"Did your dad make it to Xerxes Yosef Zachariah?" Grace asked brightly, then sipped her coffee.

"Nope. After my sister and me, he decided two children were enough for any family. Now, Alex said your last name was

Stillwater. You don't happen to be Hal's little girl, do you?"

Grace stood up tall, straightened her shoulders, then playfully stood on her tiptoes, leaning into Alex to try and squeeze another half-inch of height. "Not so little anymore. I'm five foot seven in my bare feet."

"Well, you're bright and bold enough to bring a true smile to my son's face. He's never brought a friend to a morning-after breakfast. Welcome to the inner circle, Grace," Papa Doc said, saluting her with his cup of coffee.

Just as she saluted back, Ben said, "Oh, puh-lease…" and turned away.

"Is he always that cheerful?" Grace whispered sarcastically.

"Don't pay any attention to him," Alex said. "We don't. He's perpetually in a bad mood."

"Oh, Gracie dear!" a woman's shrill voice called from afar.

Grace dropped her cup, stepping back so she didn't get splashed. "Mother!" she hissed, then realized only Alex and Papa Doc had heard her guttural reaction of disgust.

Now it was Alex's turn to give her arm a squeeze of reassurance. He pulled her close and at the same time, looked to his father. "We might need some help here, Dad."

"Don't worry. I've known Victoria for years." He turned to Grace and whispered. "No offense, but she's a pain!"

"You have no idea," Grace whispered back, then stood up tall to face her intimidator, knowing she had at least two strong men at her back. No need to fear the fists today. At least, right now.

Victoria was adorned in the classiest workout wear available, but her hair and makeup were styled for an evening soiree. She behaved as if she was ready for a run on the beach – reaching up and stretching before making her final approach – but Grace and probably everyone else knew she was here to make a social appearance.

"I was sorry to hear you suddenly got ill last night," Victoria said. She lunged forward to stretch her leg, and the sudden movement in her direction caused Grace to take a step back.

A quick smile of domination flitted across Victoria's face at the fear shown. "I hope these wonderful men took good care of you," the caustic matriarch said, adding a wink to Alex.

Alex clenched his jaw, silently counted to three, but before he had composed himself enough to say a word, his father stepped in and took control. "I think it may have been a bit of food poisoning," Papa Doc said. "I insisted she stay the night. I take it Silas got the word to you?"

Now it was Victoria's turn to take a step back. "Oh, yes, he did. I hope I'm not intruding," she said, looking at the spread of food.

"Oh, no, no, no." Papa Doc took Victoria by the inner elbow, sternly but politely leading her away from the young couple and toward the chef making omelets to order. "Let's see what we can put together for you."

Papa Doc felt an inner glow of hope. Until Victoria showed up, it looked like Alex and Grace were only pausing for sustenance, ready to go back to the garden house and enjoy the weekend with each other. He'd been hoping for a solid relationship for Alex with a single woman. Grace was quite young but seemed to be down-to-earth; not flighty like women twice her age. Yes, he'd do whatever needed to keep Victoria the Viper away from the young couple and their blossoming relationship. He didn't know how much time he had left, but if he could be a grandpa before he died, his life would be complete.

Alex set his hand gently on Grace's shoulder and whispered in her ear, "Do you want to just grab a few pastries and take off? We can go anywhere you'd like. Maybe lunch on the Seine?"

"No passport. How about somewhere closer?" Grace looked to the garden house and grinned, then heard her mother's cackling laugh. "But not too close."

"Motorcycle, car, boat, or helicopter?" he asked.

"Really? I mean, how about helicopter? And how long until a pilot shows up?"

Alex used the silver tongs to add two croissants and a few pieces of roast beef and cheddar to his plate. “You’re looking at him, sweetie.”

Grace let go of his elbow and picked up a plate. “Oh, I am so ready to leave.” She grabbed two cream cheese Danishes and said, “Now all I need is a cup of coffee to go.”

“Whoop, whoop!” Alex said, mimicking a helicopter’s rotor. “I sure didn’t see this happening when I got my arm twisted into coming here last night. Best guilt trip ever.”

“Ditto!”

***

Alex rolled off of Grace. “I’m sorry. Sort of. I really hadn’t meant to get anything started. It’s just… Damn, woman! You’re putting off some extra strong vibes or pheromones or something!”

“You have something going on there, too,” Grace said, then started to chuckle. *Yeah, if I keep you in bed or at least wanting to have sex with me, I won’t have to go back to my mother.* Her smile and her mirth evaporated as soon as she realized if she left her mother, she’d be giving up on her father and Sally, too.

“All right,” Alex said, then took a quick drink of water from the bedside table. “First, what was so funny, and then how come it got so *unfunny* all of a sudden?”

Grace brought her chin up and decided she was done with lying. She wouldn’t – couldn’t – tell him everything, but what she told him would be the truth.

“Do you promise not to kick me out of bed – or at least your life – if I tell you a secret?”

“Cross my heart, hope to go broke…”

“You’re so silly. That’s one of the many characteristics I like about you.” She took a deep breath, shut her eyes so she wasn’t looking at him, and said, “My mother set us up. Or she kinda sorta made me at least try to seduce you. But…”

“Yeah, so,” Alex said, then put his hand on her cheek. “Look at me.”

Grimacing with embarrassment, Grace opened one eye and saw his concern, then opened her other eye.

"But," he prompted.

"But I didn't think I was going to like you. At least this much. You're a blast to be around. I mean, I have – or had – a boyfriend, and I'm pals with lots of guys at school, but you're nothing like them."

"I hope I have a few years of maturity on them. I'm sure most of them will grow up eventually. So, does this mean you're hanging around with me because you want to now, and not because your mother wants you to? It was kind of obvious when she dropped by that she was making sure the mouse had taken the bait."

"You, my dear friend," Grace said, crisscrossing the curly hairs on his chest, "are not a mouse. You are more of a man than I thought I could ever have. So, now that I've said that, did I just cook the goose that laid the golden egg? Are you going to take me for a quick trip in your helicopter, and then I'll never hear from you again?"

"Nope."

"I mean, you'll probably have someone send me a Christmas card..."

"Grace, I'd like to spend Christmas Eve with you. I'm not a gambling man, but unless the world comes crashing down around us, I don't see any reason why we can't spend Christmas week in Sydney then sailing the warm waters toward Tahiti."

"Or making snowmen in Tahoe?"

"Tahoe or Tibet or wherever you want. But I really would like to take off before it gets too late. I can't fly at night yet. That's another level of certification. I was going to take a few more hours of class, but I think I just found another passion. Flying will have to wait."

Chapter 6
Ben the Broken Broker

Sunday morning

Alex received the call just moments after they had taken off. Grace could only hear one side of the conversation, but the scowl on his face made it clear that he'd received bad news. He turned the helicopter back to his starting point and set it down.

"That was the quickest touch and go I've ever made. I'm sorry about this. There's been a disaster at the job site. If there was any way I could get out of it, I would. This is too big to pass on to the job supervisor. My reputation as an architect and engineer, and the integrity of my company are at stake. Plus, the safety of the building's other wing might have been compromised with the collapse, and I might lose a few million bucks by missing a deadline… Promise me we can continue this weekend later?"

"I'm not going anywhere. At least, I hope you'll allow me to stay in the garden house. I sure don't want to go back to 'her!'"

"You can stay there, or you can have my suite at the big house. I'd rather you were there where my father can look out for you, though. Silas has been spending a lot of time with the old man lately. He's a good bouncer when need be. Both of them know your mother and will isolate you from 'her.' Besides, I think my dad has a little crush on you."

"If he does, it's a daddy crush. I've seen it before. He only had sons, right?"

"Yes, you're right. He's really excited about having you in the family," Alex said, then closed his eyes tight and groaned softly. "I mean…"

"No explanation required. I think we're both in happy shock. Don't spoil it with making excuses. Let's just go with the flow."

"Works for me. Just know that I'm a raging river right now. There's not a dam in the world that could stop me. But I do have to put everything on pause."

"Understood. And just for the record, I have those same surging, rushing feelings for you."

"No dam built…" Alex said, then paused, waiting for her to finish his thought.

"Could stop this feeling," she continued, then tiptoed up and kissed him. "I'll be waiting for you. Be safe."

***

Two days later

Back at the garden house to grab a change of clothes, Grace stopped looking through the colorful row of jogging suits to answer the door.

The chronically cranky and dour brother was there, dressed in a cable knit sweater and beige pleated slacks, a captain's hat on his shaved head. "Alex told me to come get you and bring you out to the job site. He felt really bad that he had to ruin your weekend and all," Ben said, his eye twitching.

Grace saw the tic but didn't know him well enough to discern whether he was lying or had a nervous disorder. It was true that Alex had felt horrible about cutting their trip short. She still didn't know if he had found out whether it was defective material – the supplier's fault – or a poor design – his fault. He'd been so busy that he hadn't had time to call. Just a few short texts of constant apologies. Maybe going to see him would help him relax and assuage his guilt.

"Don't worry about grabbing an overnight bag. I think he already has everything you need," Ben said, then turned away and whispered, "Hanging between his legs."

Grace glanced up and saw Ben's reflection in the mirror. She quickly looked away as soon as she saw what he had said. The last thing she needed was this weirdo finding out she had seen what he said.

"Oh, I'd like to stop in at the big house and say goodbye to your father and Silas," Grace said, looking around the room to see if she was forgetting something. She spotted her new sunglasses and grabbed them. "One more thing. I'll be right out," and went into the bathroom.

For no other reason than she had watched a parody of horror movies with her two favorite old men the night before – Papa Doc and Uncle Silas - Grace decided to leave a note just in case something weird was going on. She found one of the many pads and pens Alex kept scattered around for inspired notes or designs on the counter.

'1105 AM Tuesday. Ben picked me up to bring me to see you. You make me so happy!' Her hand twitched as she started to sign it. "Ah, what the heck." *'Love, Gracie.'*

"Is everything okay in there?" Ben asked.

Chills ran up Grace's arms at his voice. He was right outside the door, listening to her use the bathroom. What kind of pervert wanted to hear a woman pee? Another shiver. There were lots of weirdos out there. Money, power, and social status had nothing to do with that part of a person's personality. Nor did how wonderful his brother was.

Grace flushed the toilet and turned on the faucet. The note was on the vanity top, in plain sight. She opened the drawer containing Alex's shaving supplies and set the notepad and pen on top of his razor, underneath his comb. He'd find the note when he least expected it. Plus, the housekeeper didn't need to see their love notes.

"I'll be out in a sec. Would you grab a couple of bottles of water for me? Grab one for yourself, too. Alex says you never know if they'll have any on the job site."

Ben bit his bottom lip in frustration. This was taking a lot longer than he thought. He wanted to slip in and out before anyone saw his car. "I'm on it," he said. *And I'll be on you soon!*

The bathroom door popped open, startling Ben as he dropped the last of the water bottles into a cloth grocery bag. Looking up, he saw Grace with her arms in the air, securing her ponytail with a bright pink scrunchy. He felt himself harden at the thought of how he'd soon be with her, holding onto her bound hands as he…

"Are you okay?" Grace asked. "You look flushed."

"No, no. I mean, yes, I'm okay. I'm just in a hurry. Stress and blood pressure, you know. Or maybe you don't know. You've never been out in the real world, have you?" Ben said, holding the bag in front of his now bulging Dockers.

"I'm young but that doesn't mean I haven't experienced some of life's ups and downs. I'm ready; are you?"

Ben nodded, holding his lips together to keep back his smirk. *Oh, I am so ready for the ups and downs…*

***

"This doesn't look like a construction site," Grace said.

Ben pulled into his assigned parking spot at the suburban apartments he'd been downsized into. "Um, I need to grab a few things," he said, his eye twitching again. "Why don't you come up and see the place?"

Warning sirens blared in Grace's head. Whether the eye tic was lying or nerves, either one was a potential danger. "No, thanks. I'll wait for you out here." Grace reached over and pushed the window button. "Is this broken?"

"No. It won't work unless the key is in. Now, I want you to come up and see my apartment. It's not as nice as the garden house, but I think you'll enjoy it."

"I'd rather wait," Grace said and smiled, hoping he didn't see that he was scaring the piss out of her.

Ben reached in his pocket and felt the small handgun. He really didn't want to resort to it yet. "Suit yourself. It's just that I was able to convince Alex to break away for an hour. He's up there waiting for you now."

Graçe leaned forward and looked around the parking lot. "I don't see his car."

"He had one of the guys on the job drop him off while I went to pick you up. I'll take off and let you two have some time together. You'd better make it quick, though. He only gets an hour, then his ride will return to take him back."

Anticipation at seeing the new love of her life overrode Grace's common sense. "Are you sure?"

"Why would I lie?" Ben said, then turned away before she could see his eye twitching again. He opened his door and stepped out. "Go ahead and stay here if you'd rather. I'll be right back. I have to tell him you didn't want to see him."

"No, don't do that," Grace said, then paused. "Hey. Why doesn't he come out?"

"Oh, dear sweet innocent," Ben said, his head shaking back and forth in mild admonishment. "That would mean he'd have to get dressed again. As I said, he only has an hour."

"Okay. If you say so."

Ben hurried toward the outside stairs, almost running to the first step, then taking them two at a time to unlock the door. He knocked on it twice, said, "We're here, Alex," then opened it.

Grace followed behind him, her face aglow with anticipation as she stepped inside.

Ben jerked her by the arm, making sure she was completely in, then slammed the door, deadbolting the extra lock with a black key.

"Where's Alex?" she asked. She looked around the living room. A cheap futon couch and cardboard moving boxes were the only furnishings. "And why did you lock the door? You aren't sticking around to watch, I hope."

"Alex is in here," he said, leading her to the bedroom. "And I won't be here to watch." He opened the door and shoved her in. "I'm here to participate," he growled.

Grace stumbled and fell to the floor, catching herself before she did a face plant. "What? What's going on?"

"This room's all set up for you. Just you. I bet you like this sort of stuff. Cuffs, whips, and bondage. I even guessed at your size and bought you a cute little outfit to wear. Not that there was much sizing required for a thong and push up bra. You can do without the boots, I suppose. I'm more of a toe man, anyhow."

Grace gasped at the array. Black leather and metal studded bands and chains hung from eyebolts in the ceiling, belts and braided twists of whips and what looked like collars were draped from the spindles of the four-poster double bed. "What? Couldn't afford a king-sized bed?" she asked in nervous fear.

"Why spend the bucks when I'll be on top of you? That's where you really belong, you know: beneath me. Quivering with anticipation. Waiting for the next lash of my whip…" Ben reached up and grabbed her ponytail and twisted, pulling her head down to his face. "If you ever want to see that big brother of mine alive, you'll do as I say. Oh, and in that department," he patted his bulging trousers with his free hand, "I'm the big brother. You are so gonna love The Dominator."

Grace pivoted away from him, then reached up and punched his elbow, bending it the wrong direction. Ben yelped and released his grip in pained reflex. "You bitch!" he screamed, swinging wildly with his undamaged arm.

"I will *not* be hurt again," she growled. "You are so wrong about me. I *hate* pain and I have no desire to be underneath you or even see your…your…dominator dick!"

"Ah, but you are fond of my brother, are you not? Did you ever wonder why you haven't heard from him? Anyone can send a text from his phone." Ben held up Alex's cellphone.

"Where is he? If you've hurt him, I swear I'll…"

"You'll what? If you want to see him, you'll do as I say."

"How do I know you haven't done something to him already? Give me some assurance and I'll comply."

Ben shrugged a shoulder, still cradling his hyperextended elbow. "Sounds reasonable. If it will make you more *accommodating…*"

He opened the closet door and kicked twice, awakening his hostage.

"Umph!"

Alex was bound and gagged; his eyes squinted in anger at

seeing his brother. His captor.

"I brought you a surprise," Ben said, then moved aside, allowing him to view Grace.

"Omph!" Alex squealed, squirming with ferocity, trying again to escape his bindings.

"I just thought it was time for a little payback. After all these years of watching my older brother - Daddy's tall, smart, and handsome pride and joy – get all the best in life, I figured it was time for him to see how I roll."

Ben turned to Grace – now aghast and pale – and grinned in delight. "Get dressed," he said, nodding to the black leather bra and thong hanging on the footboard. "But first, strip slowly. I want to watch both you and dear brother squirm."

Alex rocked back and forth, grunting in renewed frustration at being bound and gagged. His hands and feet were numb, his neck and jaw a cold, dull ache. No doubt Ben would shoot him before his jealousy-fueled revenge was complete. How else could he get rid of the evidence of kidnap and rape? Whether he lost his hands and feet didn't matter now. He'd chew through his brother's neck if he had to. What he had to do was spare Grace. He'd heard the rumors that Ben's movie library was stacked with videos of bondage and sadism. He couldn't wait to see if his brother would try to re-enact the perversions. He had to try to do something.

"Ooh, look at his wiggle," Ben said, then kicked at Alex again.

"Leave him alone," Grace said, rushing forward to intercede.

"Nuh, uh, uh," Ben said, pulling the gun from his trouser pocket. "You wouldn't want to make love to me with his brains all spattered over the walls, would you?"

"I'll never make love to you!" Grace hissed. She paused, realizing her voice was all she had left. "Help! Rape! Fire!"

Ben put the pistol back in his pocket so he could use both hands, then tackled Grace to the bed. He shoved his forearm over her throat, throttling her, choking off both her breath and ability to scream. "If you make one more noise above a whisper, I'll shoot you and make him watch. You do know what necrophilia is, don't you?"

Alex had been stunned by the attack on his girlfriend, the woman he had decided to marry. Now that her life was on the line, his protective instincts were back, recharged with more adrenaline. He pitched himself forward and rolled towards the bed as his brother lectured.

"Necrophilia," Ben explained, his voice deepening with the excitement of being all-powerful, "is having sex with a corpse. Abuse of a corpse they call it if you get caught. Of course, I have plans for both of you. They'll never find your remains. I'm going to get big bucks for this movie." He looked up at the video camera mounted on a tripod in the corner. "Not only bondage but a snuff movie, too. That ought to be enough to finance a fresh start in Thailand. I understand they're a lot more flexible in their sexual mores. Lots of movie opportunities for an experienced director and producer. And well-hung American actor."

Grace gasped and sputtered, trying to catch a breath as he held her down. "Oh, I don't want to stifle you yet," he said, pulling his arm away just enough for her to breathe. "We have to get you aroused and satisfied before we get rid of you."

"Why?" Grace whispered hoarsely.

"Why? Revenge, of course. Don't you know that success is the best revenge there is? I plan on making more money than either of my brothers. Not that Chuck is worth a dime. That faggot does nothing but work in free clinics and give away all he owns. You see, rumor is that the old man is ready to kick the bucket. Haven't you noticed how gray he is? He's eaten up with cancer. I'll be the successful son now, even if I live in another country. I guess it doesn't matter whether I get an inheritance from him or not. As long as Alex doesn't, I'll be happy. He already has too much of everything. Including you."

Grace couldn't hear Alex struggle, so he was either passed out – unlikely – or up to something. She needed to keep Ben talking. "So, does that mean that you don't want Alex around anymore? What are you going to do with him? He's bigger than you. That's a lot to haul away."

"I told you," Ben hissed in her face, his spittle of rage sprinkling her, making her flinch. "I'm bigger, not him!"

"Haven't you heard," Grace said, an ethereal calm coming over her at the prospect of rescue by her bound lover, "that bigger isn't better? A woman craves tenderness."

Ben's face flushed with anger. He sat up and straddled Grace, then bent forward, his arms pushing her shoulders deep into the bed. "You know what? I really don't care what you or any other woman wants. All I care about is me! Why haven't you figured that out yet?"

Grace panted in renewed fear, his firmness on her belly, her arms pinned by the pressure to her shoulders. She was immobile.

But he was also fully dressed and so was she. Those two impediments would allow Alex time to rescue her before she was raped. Or he was murdered.

"Oh, you think I didn't hear my *little* brother coming up behind me?" Ben sneered, then hopped off of Grace and the bed. He kicked at Alex, knocking him from his belly crawl position onto his back like an upturned turtle bound in duct tape and rope. "There. You'll have a better view that way. Strip, woman. Now! And make it worth my while or I'll start making a bloody mess out of his miserable body."

"No, no! You're better than this, Ben," Grace pled, her hands up in supplication. "Please don't. This situation is recoverable. We can get you help. You're just under a lot of stress. Your business might be in trouble but your father…"

Ben's fist flew out and punched Grace in the mouth as the word father began to form, her plea ended with the solid tooth-loosening smack.

Alex rolled back over, the gag in his mouth tighter with his struggles. "Don't you listen, boy!" Ben hollered, kicking him onto his back again. This time he left his booted foot on Alex's throat. "It wouldn't take much to finish you off, but I want you to watch."

"Leave him alone! I'll do whatever you want. Just let him live. No. I mean, let him live whole. Don't hurt him. We'll both keep this whole fias…event a secret. Please."

Tears fell from Grace's face, her fear and begging giving Ben the sexual arousal he craved. This was better than he had ever dreamed. It wasn't some old hag his brother was involved with. This one was young, barely broke in. She might even still be a teenager. His cock grew harder at the thought.

"You're mine," he hissed, then stomped on Alex's throat, shutting out the noisome grumbles and whimpers his brother still managed to make. "No distractions. Even if he doesn't get to watch a live performance, I'll set it on auto replay. He can watch me plow your sweet little pussy until he draws his last breath…"

Thunk! Crash! Slam!

"What in the hell is going on here?"

Ben screeched, "Chuck?" then scrambled to his feet.

Grace rolled off the bed and onto the floor, furiously grasping at the duct tape and rope that bound Alex. Her fingers couldn't find a weak spot, so she jumped up and ran to the kitchen. Just about everyone in the world had a knife in there.

Suddenly, she was aware of loud voices, contentious yelling and body thunks as the two men fought. She didn't care. Grace had one mission: get Alex unbound so he could breathe. "Finally!" she huffed, grabbing a steak knife from the scatter of silverware in a kitchen drawer. She rushed into the bedroom, ducking just as Ben swung wide, missing the hero, the momentum causing the sadist to fall backward.

"I got you, Alex," Grace soothed, ignoring the fist falls and thuds, her fingers searching for a spot to slip the knife under. "Ah, crap." She turned his blue face to the side and began sawing atop his duct-taped neck, trying not to go all the way through to his skin.

"Here, let me," the stranger said, then whipped out his own

knife and deftly sliced through the cut Grace had started. He ripped the tape away, then turned Alex's head back and began mouth-to-mouth resuscitation.

"Do you know CPR?" he asked between breaths.

"No, but I'll try," she said.

"Not yet," he replied, then handed her the knife. "Cut."

Grace bent to the task of slicing through yards of duct tape and twisted nylon rope, glad for the diversion the task gave her but frustrated that she couldn't do more. When she got up to unbind his other side, she glanced around the small apartment, looking for Ben. He was laid out on the floor by the front door, his leg askew. It was either broken or his knee was trashed – or both. Her assailant's mouth hung open, his chest rising and falling slowly. Knocked out but not dead. Either way, he wasn't going anywhere on his own power.

"Did you call 911?" she asked.

"Would you? There has to be a phone around here somewhere."

Grace laid Alex's hands out straight, hoping the sudden rush of blood didn't injure them further. Her initial search for the phone was cautious - she didn't want to disturb anything that might be evidence – then suddenly became desperate. Lamps and boxes were knocked over as she looked for a phone.

"Check the walls for the outlet," the man said, then he bent back to breathing for Alex. "If you can't find it, run to a neighbor's. He's in rough shape."

Grace looked at every wall outlet but when she finally found the one for a phone line, it was empty. "I'll be right back," she said. "And thanks."

She knocked on three doors before anyone answered. "Yes," the older woman drawled, then looked up and saw Grace's battered face. "Oh, my. Are you all right?"

"No," Grace said, then shoved her way past the concerned crone. "Where's the phone? My friend needs an ambulance."

"Right there on the counter, dear. Help yourself, but please don't make any long distance…

Grace tuned out the woman as she dialed emergency services. "Yes, ma'am. I need an ambulance. No, I don't know the address, but it's two doors down from the one I'm calling from. Just send the medics and I'll wait in the parking lot and show them which apartment. Please hurry. Yes. His name is Alexander Armstrong. Shoot, I don't know his medical history. He's been strangled. Someone's up there giving him CPR right now. No, I don't want to hold. There's nothing I can tell you other than his name. Yes, go ahead and send a police officer, too. Yes, there was a crime committed. I just hope it wasn't murder."

Chapter 7
Chuck the Invisible

"There's nothing more we can do for him now," the man said as they watched the ambulance pull away, wishing he could reach out and comfort her. "Damn! I wish I'd been here sooner!"

"I'm sorry. Who are you?"

"Don't be sorry," he replied, wiping away his tears. "I'm Chuck. The other brother. The one no one talks about."

"You gave mouth-to-mouth to one brother and beat the snot out of the other?" Grace remarked, then snorted in disbelief. "Um, I think they're going to be talking about you for a long time."

Chuck laughed and shook his head. "I doubt it. Actually, I prefer a low profile. I take it you're Grace."

"How'd you know?"

"I may not be tight with my brothers, but Dad and I are close. The other two just don't pay attention to us. Alex is a workaholic and partier who just found the love of his life. And Ben is the investment broker who is always going after the next bigger, better stock or IPO, then brooding for months when it doesn't pan out."

"Actually, from what little I know about Ben, you're being quite generous in your description." Grace paused. "Wait! You said Alex just found the love of his life. You mean me?"

"Duh! He and I didn't get a chance to talk after he met you, but Dad and Silas went on and on about how they've never seen him so happy. Actually, they were both concerned and that's why I'm here."

"I was wondering about that…"

"It seems that no one has heard from Alex for two days. I know he has one of those new cellphones that can send messages like a pager."

"Yes. He gave me one, too. I left it at the house. He sent me a few text messages, but he never called me."

"Yup. That's what Dad said, too. That doesn't sound like him. I called his office and they said he had a new girlfriend and would be incommunicado for a week. That didn't sound like him, either. New girlfriends are usually bored wives and never last more than a few hours at a time."

Grace raised her eyebrows but remained mute.

"Sorry. That was probably too much information. So, missing brother number one and mystic message on my answering machine from brother number two."

"What was the message?"

"'Do you know where I can get a hurry-up passport and visa to Thailand? Something's just come up.' That meant to me that he was probably in trouble with the securities exchange commission again and had to leave the country. I came over here to see if I could help. I certainly didn't find what I expected!"

"Do you think he's going to be okay? I mean, can we go to the hospital and wait there?"

Chuck looked up and saw the apartment door was open, police tape draped across it. "Let me make sure they don't have any more questions for me. Or you. You don't mind if I speak for both of us, do you?"

"Actually, I'd appreciate it. I don't know what I'm doing."

Chuck reached up and touched her forehead. "A little clammy. You might be in shock. We'll get some fluids in you; maybe a little juice or soda. The sugar will do you good. Wait here."

Grace glanced up at the apartment and got a shiver. "Yeah, staying here's fine."

A short minute later, Chuck was back. "I gave him my number and said he could contact both of us there."

Her back straightened in terror at Chuck's words. He noticed it and changed his approach. "I gave him my pager number. I figure we'll both be at the hospital until Alex is out of trouble. After that, I hope you plan on staying with Dad. That is unless you have another place. Sorry, I don't know anything about you other than everyone who meets you is infatuated with you."

“I’m beginning to hate the word infatuated.”

“Well, Ben’s screwed no matter what. I don’t think you’ll ever have to worry about him. I don’t think there’s a death sentence in this state for kidnapping or attempted murder, but a life sentence sounds like a definite possibility.”

“Or life in a mental institution.”

“I pity the poor doctors there,” Chuck said, then nodded to the dinged and faded van. “My chariot awaits.”

“You’re sure you’re part of this family?” Grace asked, suddenly wary. Then she remembered how he had just come in and literally saved the day for her. “But even if you’re not, thanks for what you did.”

“I had about twenty years of getting-even punches pent up. It was definitely my pleasure. I just wish I’d been here sooner.”

Grace accepted his help getting in, then reached out and put her hand on his forearm. “I’m just glad you weren’t a minute later.”

Chuck gasped and straightened up as he realized what he could have walked in on. “Oh, Lord. I didn’t even think of it that way…”

“Come on.” Grace pulled the seatbelt across her and clicked it in. “Let’s get to the hospital.”

***

“We can go through this way,” Chuck said, leading her through the emergency room, past the nurses’ station.

“Hey, Baby Doc! What are you doing on this side of town?”

“Slummin’!” Chuck answered back, slapping his hand down on the counter and grinning. “Nah, I got someone special in here I want to see.”

“Hey, is that your girlfriend?” one of the younger nurses asked.

“Maybe,” he said, then touched Grace’s elbow. “Play along,” he whispered, then led her through the corridor.

As soon as they were out of earshot, Grace pulled away. “Play along?” she asked. “What? Who?”

“You’re going to hear about it sooner or later,” Chuck said, looking around to make sure they were alone. He saw the chapel and pulled her into it. “I’m gay but still in the closet, shall we say. A few of the nurses have been hitting on me. Actually, both male and female nurses. If I pretend to have a girlfriend, both groups will leave me alone.”

“Groups? You have groups of nurses hitting on you?”

“Not really groups. Let’s just say factions. I think they’re all just fishing, trying to get me to come out one way or the other.”

“Sorry, Chuck, but I’ve led a very sheltered life. I’ve read some stories about gay people. You’re just regular folks with yens for the same gender, right?”

“Wow. That’s blunt. Blunt but accurate.”

“Yeah, well, you should hear my mother rant and rave about how queers are ruining America. I figured if she was that adamant about it, something had to be wrong.” Grace looked around the small chapel and saw the clock. “Do you think he’s out of surgery now?”

“If they had to perform surgery, he’s probably still there. Or at least, in post-op. The only thing he might have needed would be a tracheotomy.” Chuck pointed to the soft spot under his Adam’s Apple. “Ben messed him up pretty good.”

“I was worried about his hands but being able to breathe is way more important.”

“Come on. I’ll see what I can find out.”

“Won’t they tell me anything?” Grace asked.

“Nope. You’re not his wife or mother or sister and probably don’t have medical power of attorney. You don’t, do you?”

“Alex and I weren’t together that long; just long enough to know that neither of us saw an end to our relationship.”

“That’s good to hear. He was due to have a good woman. At least, one he didn’t have to share…Sorry, that was crass. I think I have a little shock going on, too.”

“Here,” Grace said, offering him her can of soda. “I’m not afraid of your cooties.”

“Yeah, being queer ain’t contagious, darling,” Chuck said, then took a long swallow of the lemon-lime soda. He handed it back to her and put a comforting arm around her shoulder. "I'll never hit on you, but right now, I need you next to me more than you'll ever know."

"Back at ya," Grace said and snuggled into him.

***

The two walked down the hall, their easy pace identical and comfortable. "So, how come everyone knows you here?" Grace asked.

"I'm a doctor. I don't operate out of here, but I do have courtesy privileges."

"Which means?"

"Which means if I ask, they'll tell. I'm not a surgeon, anyhow. I mean, I can cut and sew, but I run a clinic on the other end of town. You know, the proverbial wrong side of the tracks?"

"Helping those who can't afford to pay?"

"Pretty much. Say, look up. See who's here?"

Papa Doc was as gray as dirty springtime snow and just as precarious as he stood up, Silas quick at his side to steady him. "Any word yet?"

"I was just going to ask you the same thing, Dad."

"And you?" Papa Doc asked Grace. His hand gently explored the side of her face where Ben had punched her. "Ouch. Looks like a good chunk of steak would help that. Did he, um, do anything else?"

"Other than just about kill Alex, no. Pretty much intimidation. He would have, though, if Chuck hadn't interceded."

Grace looked up and saw Chuck in a different light. Yes, he was still the tall, good-looking man who had come to the rescue, but he also looked like a younger version of his father. All the men in the family had broad shoulders, strong jawlines, and bright blue eyes, but Alex had darker hair and a more robust nose. Chuck's nose was finer, almost feminine. She shuddered as she started to consider Ben, then blocked him out. He couldn't bully her anymore, even as a memory. She wouldn't allow it.

"Are you all right?" Chuck asked, feeling her falter. He squeezed her close again. "We have you: Dad, Silas, and me. And Alex when he gets better. All of us are here for you. You know that, right?"

Grace nodded, the tears starting to slip out. "I just want this day to be over. I want to go back in time to three days ago…"

"Oh, Gracie! Hello, Gracie, dear!"

Grace slumped at the sound of her mother's voice. She looked up at Chuck. "Tell me I'm hallucinating. That isn't my mother, is it?"

Chuck looked up at the ultra-thin woman walking down the hall, rushing but trying to look like she was on a catwalk, one foot placed in front of the other in a practiced manner. "It's a woman, but nothing about her reminds me of you."

"Yeah, that's her mother," Silas said. "Put on your shit boots."

Papa Doc and Grace both sniggered into their hands, then looked at each other, comfortable in their identical reaction to Silas's spot-on declaration.

"Boots on, strapped, and tied," Chuck said softly through a clenched smile as he watched the woman approach. He gave Grace a quick cuddle of assurance then waited for the drama that was sure to come.

"Gracie, darling. Where have you been? I went to the Armstrong's to see if you'd recovered. I was sure you'd be better by now."

Chuck looked down, his movement causing Grace to look up. She had a moment of clarity, realizing this woman had nothing on her now. "Why are you here, Mother?"

"Oh…I…ahem. I thought that if you were severely sick, you would have been admitted to the hospital."

"You could have called," Grace said, her voice icy. "Certainly, they would have told a mother if her daughter was a patient; no medical power of attorney required."

Victoria gasped at the remark, surprised that her little girl – so easily intimidated four days ago – was suddenly secure and independent. Or at least had found no less than three strong men to protect her. "Oh, and your little friend Dusty came by looking for you," she lied, an evil glint in her eye. *Don't mess with me, Missy! I can still play dirty.*

Grace tensed, held her breath, then let it out. "That's funny," Grace lied back. "I talked to him just yesterday. He said he joined the army because his dad got a new job upstate. I wished him well and that was that. Are you sure it was Dusty who called?" *I know you're lying. Get out of my life and out of my head!*

"Actually," Victoria said, strutting over to sit next to Papa Doc, "I heard that Alex had been involved in an accident. He didn't crash his helicopter, did he?"

Papa Doc and Silas looked at each other, wondering how she could know Alex was in the hospital. A smile started to bloom on Silas's face. "You've been talking to Jimmy, haven't you?" he asked.

"Well, I may have met him at coffee this morning…" Victoria said, a sudden blush rising to show through her three layers of foundation.

"Victoria, Victoria, Victoria," Papa Doc said condescendingly, patting her hand like she was a six-year-old. "You have to quit following after the *paparazzi*. You'll get more gray hairs than Lady Clairol can keep up with." He looked at her temple, noticing the telltale smear of a recent dye job that hadn't been completely cleaned up. "All is fine here. It was just a little incident. Nothing major. Grace has agreed to stay at the house and keep him company while he recovers."

"What happened?" Victoria asked.

Chuck stepped in. "That's private," he said. "Family only. Now, if you don't mind, I had asked everyone here for a family meeting and we were just getting started."

"And who are you?" Victoria snapped. Her eyes widened as she realized that he looked just like Papa Doc had thirty years ago.

"You're not..."

"Oh, yes, I am. I'm Chuck, the youngest Armstrong son." He moved away from Grace, nudging her gently, nodding toward Silas and his father. "So, now that you've seen Grace is in good hands, I'm sure you'll allow us a little privacy." He put his elbow out, enjoining her wordlessly to follow him.

Grace sat between the two older men, one hand on each man's arm, clutching them with her fingertips until Chuck and her mother were out of sight. She lay her head on Papa Doc's shoulder, ready to share. "I think I need to tell you something," she said softly.

"You mean that your mother set you up with Alex; that it wasn't your idea to come to the party?"

"Did Alex tell you?" she asked, sitting up straight with surprise sprinkled with irritation.

"Sweetheart," Papa Doc said, "that's the way things go in this crazy world. Whether rich or poor, mothers have been setting up their daughters with good 'finds' for centuries. She's no different than any other mother."

"Well, maybe," Silas and Grace said at the same time. Silas nodded to her, urging her to continue.

Grace shrugged. "She's horrid. I came to the event under duress. She threatened my friend Dusty. Or rather, she threatened me with what she'd do to Dusty and his father if I didn't do what she said."

"And the other thing you're not telling me?" Papa Doc asked. He turned her head to the side and traced over the yellowing bruise. "If I'm not mistaken, this is a woman's handprint and it's a few days old. That means she physically and emotionally coerced you into crashing the party."

Grace nodded, the tears spilling as she relived the horror of her mother threatening to rape her with a wine bottle and blame it on Dusty and his father if she didn't obey her. "Why couldn't it have been her, not Alex? She doesn't deserve to live and he does."

"He'll be fine," Silas soothed, then looked up. "Here comes

Chuck. Maybe he found something out."

Chuck saw the apprehension in the men's eyes and the tears on Grace's cheeks. That meant they hadn't heard anything about Alex yet, but also that Grace had just revealed something intense. "Remember, Grace," he said, kneeling down in front of her, "We're here for you."

"You know what's the worst part? I've lost my father. I mean, he's not dead, but I can't get to him without going through her."

"Don't worry about him," Silas said. "In case you haven't heard, I'm the miracle worker when it comes to social *imbroglios*. I'll get in touch and let him know whatever you want to share or where you want to meet. *And* I'll hold back whatever you want to keep private. It looks like I'm going to have to have another talk with Jimmy and his new assistant. He'll get nothing if he starts playing me against Victoria."

"Wow. This really is a different world," Grace said, wiping her tears with the cloth Silas offered.

"And now you know why I keep away," Chuck said so softly, he was certain the men wouldn't hear him.

Grace looked up at him and winked. "And I'm here for you, too."

***

"How long have we been here?" Grace asked, suddenly awake from the nap she hadn't planned on taking.

Chuck rubbed his eyes and looked down at his watch. "Almost three hours. Something's not right here. We should have received an update." He unwrapped his arm from around her shoulders and sat up. "Excuse me a minute while I check this out."

Grace watched as he walked away, stretching his arms, working the kinks out of his neck and shoulders from holding her close.

"Yeah, he's a keeper," Silas said. "No disrespect to his dad, but two out of three ain't bad when it comes to having stellar kids. I don't know what went wrong with Ben. He never was wired right. Even as a kid, he'd torment cats and dogs, and even his little brother. Alex was always there for Chuck, though. Stepping in, thrashing him like brothers do when someone's picking on a kid brother. Didn't make any difference to him whether it was his own brother or a neighbor kid."

"Why should it?" Papa Doc asked, now awake. "I mean, it was a straightforward case of the big beating on the little. That's probably one reason Chuck has such a big heart. He didn't have a younger sibling to protect. He learned how to do it from Alex and transferred that skill to taking care of the poor folks on the other side of town."

Silas patted Papa Doc on the shoulder. "Now, now. Don't cut yourself short. You had a little influence on that, too."

"Are you a real doctor?" Grace asked. "I mean, I thought folks were calling you Papa Dog at first, not Papa Doc."

Both men laughed. "Yes, I was a doctor. I guess I still am if the need arises. I haven't practiced in ten years, at least. My health started going downhill, so I decided to slow down. You know, get rid of the stress."

"Plus, it's not as if you had to work," Silas said.

Papa Doc glared at his words, then he relaxed and sat back. "Well, if she's going to be family, she might as well know. I still have a few bucks stashed away in the Old Money piggy bank. I kept pulling more and more out of it, trying to keep Ben from going under. Alex would put more back in every time he got a chance. It's not as if it was near empty, but he finally took me aside and explained it so it made sense. Ben would never grow up and take responsibility for his screw-ups if we kept bailing him out. He'd keep sticking his finger in the blades as long as we kept pulling the fan back. We had to walk away so he'd know that if he stuck it in there again, it was going to hurt."

Chuck walked in on the conversation, ready to add, "Ben's just an ass," then decided it was best to stay still. He sat down on the other side of his father and leaned back, trying to make some sense out of how messed up the day had become.

“So, he got mad and decided he’d make Alex pay?” Grace asked. “He not only wanted him to hurt physically but emotionally, too. From what you all have told me, I’m the first real…um…lady friend Alex has had any interest in.”

“Excuse me,” a man in blue scrubs said. “You are the Armstrong’s, right?” he asked.

Chuck sat up straight, then stood up, nodding to the surgeon.

“Oh, hi, Chuck. I didn’t see you there. Shoot! Was Alex your brother?”

“Was?” Grace gasped, then fell back in the chair, glad she hadn’t been standing. She held her hand over her mouth, willing herself not to puke, her breathing slow and deliberate.

“Shit,” the surgeon huffed. “I’m sorry. I’m really, really sorry. We did everything we could. He was on a breathing machine. We thought everything was going to be fine, and then his blood pressure went sky high. It was a stroke.”

Chuck focused on his father’s face as the surgeon spoke the words. He’d had a three-second heads-up that Alex had passed. He wasn’t psychic, but he had seen the grief in the doctor’s eyes when he came out, looking for the next of kin. It would have been worse if he had asked everyone into a private room. That would only have prolonged the agony for everyone, including the surgeon.

His father was in shock. They’d better get him to a room right away. He knew he had finished chemo the week before, but he wasn’t totally out of the woods. “Can we get him a bed?” Chuck asked the surgeon, nodding to his father. “I want to make sure he’s doing okay.”

“Oh, yeah. Of course. Let’s go down the hall to the ER. I’ll grab a wheelchair.”

The combination of the two stresses – losing Alex and watching Papa Doc falter before her eyes – was too much. Grace grabbed the trash can next to her and lost her resolve to keep it all together, puking up streams of bile and soda, her shoulders heaving, nose running as she broke down sobbing without caring who saw her.

"Make that a double room and two wheelchairs," Silas called out, rushing to Grace with a box of tissues.

Chapter 8
Recuperating

Late June 1991

"Are you sure it isn't the flu?" Grace asked Papa Doc.

"You're the one who came to me. Have you taken a pregnancy test yet?"

"Yeah, well, you know those things aren't that accurate," she said, then sighed in resignation and shook her head. "Now what?"

"Looks like you get to make me a grandpa," he said.

"But there was one other. I mean, it wasn't just Alex."

"You mean Chuck?" he asked, then laughed. "Now that would really be a miracle."

Grace glared at him, trying to keep her resolve, then giggled at the inside joke. She had been living with Chuck as boyfriend and girlfriend to the outside world, but as brother and sister to those who knew them.

"Ben never got to you, did he?" he asked, suddenly concerned. "Because if he did, I'm gonna whack that spaghetti noodle dick of his off at the base."

"They wouldn't let you into prison to do that," Chuck said. "Sorry, I didn't mean to eavesdrop. You just didn't hear me come in."

"Yes, I did," Papa Doc said. "She didn't, though."

"Little Miss Superwoman ears didn't hear me? She must have been distracted," Chuck said, then leaned over and gave her a quick kiss.

Grace grinned at the kiss, then pouted again. "Yes, I was distracted. I think I'm pregnant."

"Of course, you're pregnant."

"What? When did you find out?" she asked.

"Duh! We live in the same house. I empty the trash occasionally, you know."

"Every day," Grace said. "You have got to be the cleanest housekeeper I've ever known. You could give Sally lessons."

"Who's she?"

"She was my nanny growing up. When my mother decided I didn't need one, she canned her. Dad knew how close I was to her, so he gave her a job as housekeeper and light cook."

"How do you cook light?" Papa Doc asked, then slapped his knee. "I still got it."

"Yeah, and I hope I don't get it," Silas said. "So, what's this I hear that I'm gonna be a grandpa?"

"You guys are making this difficult for me," Grace said in a huff.

"Honey," Papa Doc said, his hand on hers. "We don't ever want to make your life difficult. On the contrary. Now, whether I am the biological grandfather of the child you're carrying or not, I am still going to claim her as mine. I mean, you're not my biological daughter, but I'd fight whoever challenged my love for you with a fistfight. Of course, I would have to try and win by intimidation first because I'm as weak as any man twice my age, but I'm certain of my love for you."

"Ditto," Silas said. "And Papa Doc and I aren't a couple but who says this little girl can't have three granddads?"

Grace's grin swished side-to-side as she tried to figure out if she wanted to laugh or cry. "Thanks for keeping my first dad in the loop. I'll let him know about it in person when he comes by on Tuesday. And please, don't anyone let my mother know. Promise me, right now, each and every one of you three, that you won't so much as let my mother touch my child. She can see a picture of him or her, but no touching. After what she did to me - and threatened me with – I couldn't…wouldn't…"

"Calm down," Chuck said. "We won't let her near you or our baby. Oh, and yes, we can get married if you'd like."

"Chuck!" Silas and Papa Doc screeched at the same time.

"That's not how you ask a woman to marry you, son," Papa

Doc said sternly.

"Tsk, tsk," Silas muttered, then returned to making cucumber sandwiches for lunch.

"What? I just wanted to let her have an easy out if she wanted," Chuck said. "Are you putting pickles on those sandwiches, Silas?"

"They're cucumber sandwiches which means they're already pickles. Or at least, could be."

"Chuck, you know I love you," Grace said. "And if I had anything but sisterly feelings for you," she rolled her eyes, "you could be my Mr. Right. However, there's a chance that this baby could be someone else's. Remember I said something to you all about my mother threatening my friend, Dusty?"

"The one you said joined the army?" Papa Doc asked.

"Well, Mother lied about him, so I did, too. I don't know where he is. Lord, I hope she didn't concoct some lie and have him and his dad thrown in jail."

"Why would she do that?" Silas asked, then set down the knife. "Oh, wait. She's Victoria Stillwater. She doesn't have to have a reason, right?"

"Yes and no," Grace said. "She's crazy, but I think she'd do it just to be mean to me."

"Why is she so mean to you?" Chuck asked.

"Because she's Victoria Stillwater," Papa Doc and Silas said at the same time.

"So, I'm pregnant, unmarried, one potential father is dead and the other is missing…" Grace sniffed, looked around for something to wipe her nose with, then realized that 'Always There For You' Chuck had a box of tissues ready.

Silas cleared his throat to bring the attention away from her as she cleaned up the physical remnants of her distress. "Yes, all that's true. One of those three statements is wonderful: the pregnancy. One is horrific: Alex is dead. The other is an unknown, totally fixable by someone I know who is a fantastic detective."

"Who's that?" Papa Doc asked. Chuck frowned as he nudged

his father and grunted. "Oh! Yeah, that would be you, right, Silas?"

"Correct. So, we have a baby coming, a fantastic support network of three mostly able-bodied men," he looked Chuck up and down, "some more so than the others, but all of us are willing to help you through this."

"But how do I keep my mother from finding out?"

Papa Doc gave her a quick squeeze. "Your father's already sneaking over here to see you once a week. I doubt we'll be able to keep your impending motherhood a secret for long. If he's been able to keep his visits a secret, I'm sure he'll be able to handle the ultimate discretion: another addition to his family tree."

"What would I do without you?" Grace asked, her tears starting anew.

"We'll never know because we'll always be here for you," Chuck said.

"As long as I have a breath left in this old body..." Papa Doc started, then corrected himself. "I guess it's a good time to tell you. I'm clear. At least, so far, so good."

Chuck smacked him on the back playfully. "Didn't I tell you that attitude made all the difference in treating cancer? All those good vibes streaming through your body kicked the bad ones out."

"And this coming from a medical professional?" Papa Doc teased. "You're right, though. So, let's get down to business. Grace, you tell Silas everything you know about Dusty and his father: friends, schools, hangouts, barber, the works. From there, he'll set out his guys. Mark my words, it won't be long and he'll be joining this family."

"Huh?" Grace asked.

"You don't think I'm going to ever give you up, do you? I own enough businesses around this country that I'm sure he'll fit in with one of them. A good manager is always in demand. At least, I still believe in nepotism."

"Nepo-what?" she asked.

"That just means he believes in hiring his relatives," Chuck said. "Except his sons were as independent as he is. Let's hope that finding family outside the bloodlines will work."

"Amen to that," Papa Doc said. "Now, what's for lunch? Only good food from now on. I'm going to take better care of my body this time around. Not everyone gets a second chance."

Grace rubbed her belly, melancholy despite the pep talk and dynamic support team surrounding her. *Eighteen, unmarried, and pregnant. If Mother knew, she'd be howling in bitter delight.*

***

Mid-July 1991

Victoria Stillwater looked over her ladies' club's bank statement again. It had been two months and he still hadn't cashed that check. Looking through the window, she wondered where that boy and his father had fled to. The new gardener was decent to watch – broad-shouldered but with that inbred flaming red hair. His manager was a pain to deal with, always wanting to be paid upfront. She'd have to call the agency and have a new landscaper sent out for next week.

She didn't know whether Dusty had believed her or not when she told him that Grace was upset, so traumatized by something that had happened the week before that she didn't want to talk about it. She alluded that it had something to do with him, adding the stinger that Grace had asked her to tell him not to ever contact her again.

Maybe saying she was so hurt that she didn't even want to bother with graduation – that she wanted a fresh start in Europe – was overkill, but she wanted Dusty completely out of Grace's life. When he insisted he could make everything right if he could just speak to her, it was time to bring out the checkbook. Money, the great negotiator.

"You seem like a nice young man. You're a hard worker. You could have a comfortable life with some college under your belt. How about I help with some tuition? Consider it an investment in your future. You can do the same for someone else when you're well off. Ten thousand dollars will get you through junior college. Keep

your grades up, and you'll be able to transfer over to a first-class university and maybe get a scholarship. Go west. Try California. There are plenty of great schools out there, plus the weather is so much nicer."

"Listen to her, son," his father had said. "Chances like this don't happen often."

Dusty slapped the check onto his palm a couple of times, pondering his future. Ten thousand dollars would be more than enough to start his own business. Lawn and garden care in the summer; snow plowing and private drive maintenance in the winter. He felt his father's hand on his, folding his fingers over the check.

"Take it, son," he asked more than instructed, biting his bottom lip, hoping his son would be able to have a better future than his.

"Thank you," Dusty said to Mrs. Stillwater, then nodded, not wanting to insult the elitist woman with a handshake from a working man.

"Well, it looks like he's still deciding what to do or he's lost the check. Damn! And here I was hoping I could get him for theft and forgery." Victoria looked over the carbon copy of the check she had written, intentionally changing the angle of her signature and misspelling her own last name. "He must have lost it. I doubt he has the balls to come back and ask for another one. At least, he's gone."

"Good afternoon, Victoria," Hal said as he walked into the den. "Checking the balances on all those bank accounts you keep?"

"How'd you know… I mean, yes, I'm doing some bookkeeping. Why do you ask?"

"Just wondering if you've heard from our daughter." Hal sat down in the recliner and held a magazine up so she couldn't see his face if he happened to break character. "I was hoping she'd send us a postcard or two. Europe in the summer can be divine."

"Oh, she called last night, just after you went to the club. She's been keeping busy with her new friends," Victoria said, then moved papers over her bank statements so he couldn't see the numbers.

"Where is she this week?" Hal asked.

"I believe she was in Paris."

"Let's see, I left at eight, so that means it was sometime after two in the morning in Paris."

"I think she may have been calling from London."

"Really, Victoria. I wish you'd let me speak with her when she calls. I miss my little girl. I don't think we've ever gone more than a week without chatting."

"Well…well," Victoria said, trying not to stutter but suddenly at a loss for words. "Well, she's getting older now. She's in Europe, with a new group of friends, and a whole new way of life."

Hal shrugged, knowing she could see his gesture but kept his National Geographic held high, his grin of glee at terrorizing her hid behind it. "Just let me know if she needs money. I can wire it to her. I don't want her going without."

"As a matter of fact," Victoria began, but Hal cut her off.

"But tell her I want postcards or a phone call first. No money until I get proof she's still alive."

"I think you're being ridiculous," Victoria huffed, frustrated that she'd once again been thwarted in getting more money out of her husband.

Hal put the magazine down and glared at her. "Ridiculous? No, I'm not," he said. "And get dressed. We're going out tonight. You committed us to an appearance at a fundraiser for the hospital. If you said we'd be there, we will."

***

"Hey, Sweetie Pie," Hal said. "Are you feeling better today?"

"Oh, Daddy," she cried, reaching out for a much-needed hug, then stopped as she felt her gorge rise. She held her hand up and ran to the bathroom.

"How long is this going to last?" Hal asked Chuck.

"Dad said each woman and each pregnancy is different. I want to get her in for an ultrasound. It's kind of hard doing it under the radar. Are you sure this is the right way to go?"

Hal nodded. "I'm going to respect Grace's wish to keep her

mother out of her life. As it is, that woman's haunting hospitals, police departments, and even insane asylums looking for her. And no telling how many private eyes she's hired."

Silas walked in, his arms loaded with groceries. "All she has to do is have the *paparazzi* sniff around."

"Oh, she has those guys eating out of her hand," Hal said. "She's spread the word that Grace has fled to the Balkans with some Romanoff heir, that the two of them are seeking the true meaning of life…or some other horseshit. Those boys aren't stupid. They're looking, but they won't print anything without a picture. Actually, she's pretty smart there. She's getting at least Jimmy and his crew for free. They're pretty thorough."

"Yup," Silas said, "and that's why we want to keep her here. No one gets into this compound without permission. She has plenty of activities to entertain her, good food," he held up a head of romaine lettuce and two large tomatoes, "fresh air…"

"And fantastic company," Grace said, completing the often-heard soliloquy on how she needed to stay put.

"Plus your dear old dad has been seeing you more now than when you were living at home! Come here and give your old man a hug," Hal said, arms opened wide as he walked toward her.

"Are you really okay?" he whispered in her ear.

She pulled out of the embrace and nodded. "If I get the urge to go shopping or talk to someone new, all I have to do is think of her coming at me, her shrill voice belittling me, or telling me how worthless my friends are."

"So, she did hit you then?" Hal asked.

Grace took a deep breath and looked at Chuck, then Papa Doc. She was done protecting her. She nodded and felt the tears come. She blinked them back. She'd never let her mother make her cry again.

"No need for details," Hal said. "I'm sure I'll find a way out of our marriage."

Silas started chuckling despite the somberness of the

conversation.

"What's so funny, Silas," Hal asked crossly. "You wouldn't be laughing if you were the one who had to see her face every morning!"

"No, you're right there. I just remembered hearing Robert Van der Cleft tell about the masseuse his wife had come make house calls. Evidently, our dear Robert has video cameras set up all over the house. Zelda knows about most of them because they're hidden just enough so she can find them and turn them off. He set her up with André the Giant."

"The wrestler? He's a masseuse?" Chuck asked.

"Not the same guy. This one is called the giant because of his monster sausage. If you'd like, I can get his number. You just figure out which room or rooms sweet little Victoria is most likely to want a *personal* massage in, and we can send him right over." Silas shifted in his shirt, slightly uncomfortable with the proposition. "On second thought, we – or I – might have to have one of her lady friends set up first. Without the camera, of course. If the idea comes from one of her confidants, she's more likely to take the bait."

"What? Are you André's pimp or something?" Chuck asked with a nervous chuckle.

"Nope," Silas said with a wide smirk. "I'm just one of the three who claim your little angel. I want Grace protected. One way to help is to get that Mad Medusa out of her life so she doesn't have to live under house arrest."

"Yeah, well, even if it is the most magnificent place on earth to be incarcerated, I still can't come and go at will. What do you say, Dad? Is it time to finally get your freedom?" Grace asked, suddenly happier than she'd been in weeks.

"Oh, yeah… Silas, let's make a plan."

***

August 1991

"There's a mobile ultrasound unit in DC, but we can't bring it here. We're going to have to sneak you out in disguise, give you an assumed name, and hope that Jimmy or one of his boys isn't watching," Papa Doc said.

"No," Grace said, then rolled back over in bed, pulling the sheet over her head.

"But honey, we need to see if there's something going on in there."

She rolled her head and shoulders back just enough to look him in the eye. "Chuck and I discussed what might be going on. He doesn't suspect anything tragic. There *would* be a tragedy, though, if she found out where I was and my condition. I only have six more months of this and then the pregnancy is over. Whether I'm having one or two babies, the health care stays the same: eat right, drink plenty of fluids, and get lots of rest. It's just the curiosity factor that will be satisfied. I won't risk it."

"But don't you want to know?"

"Of course I want to know, but I don't want my mother in my face gloating. She'd find a way to claim credit for me being so fertile..." Grace paused, then groaned in defeat. "She already claimed credit. As soon as she found out I had sex, she said I was pregnant; that women in her family were ultra-fertile or something like that. Great. I can't even claim or blame being pregnant without her interference."

"How's my girl doing?" Chuck asked, joining the conversation when he heard Grace's refusal to get an ultrasound.

"Still pregnant," she said, then reached for the trash can. She coughed up the little bit of lunch she had managed to eat, then set the can back down. "Sorry."

"No worries," Chuck said. He pulled out the plastic trash can liner, added it to the sealed trash receptacle in the closet, then relined her barf bucket. "And still pregnant is a good thing. Don't worry about getting an ultrasound. You're right: nothing's going to change on the number of babies. Women have been having twins for eons without tests. Pretty soon, I'll be able to hear one heartbeat or two. I am concerned, though, about your nausea. I did a little research on traditional remedies for morning sickness."

"You mean you asked some of the ladies who come in to see you at the clinic?" Papa Doc suggested.

"Research, local consultants, *kaffeeklatsch* group: same thing. It seems the best remedy is not legal yet but very prevalent and effective. Now, I know you don't care for smoking, but until you can get your tummy settled down enough to eat some Alice P. Toklas brownies, you'll have to take a puff or two." Chuck pulled a joint out of his shirt pocket. "Courtesy of some of Plymouth's finest."

"You mean, smoke it in here?" Grace asked, elbowing her way up to a seated position, getting a burst of energy at the prospect of finding a cure for her nausea.

"Sure, why not? Who's going to bust you? Dad?"

"Nope, not me," Papa Doc said. "Oh, and it's B. Toklas, not P. Toklas."

The window halfway lifted open, Chuck stopped and looked back. "Dad?"

"You didn't know I had baking skills, did you, son? How do you think I got through three rounds of chemo? After you take a puff - maybe two - Grace, let me have that doobie. I don't want you to get plastered. If you've never smoked, it might knock you on your butt."

"I'm already knocked on my butt," Grace said. "Would you start this, Papa Doc. I don't know what I'm doing."

"I thought you'd never ask," he said, then pulled a lighter out of his pocket. "I was hoping you'd figure this out by yourself, Chuck. I've been wanting to suggest it for weeks but didn't know if her doctor would approve."

"Well, as her doctor," Chuck said, "I did both field and medical research. She's in more danger by not smoking and becoming dehydrated and malnourished than inhaling a little smoke with cannabinoids. Plus, when I asked one of the mothers if she got morning sickness with her children, she said, 'Every time.' She said smoking a little weed to start the day settled her tummy plus made managing her crew of eight a lot easier."

"Eight? Oh, no way am I going through this again. And I'm not even halfway through the pregnancy!"

"Hold it like this," Chuck said, then lit the end of the marijuana cigarette, and inhaled. "Wow! It's been a long time…" he said while holding his breath, then exhaled and handed it to her.

Grace took a novice-sized puff but swallowed the smoke rather than inhaled it. "That wasn't too bad."

"Yeah, well, you didn't pull it into your lungs," Papa Doc said. "Here, watch me."

He demonstrated, then looked up and saw Silas in the doorway. His eyes widened but he didn't lose breath control. He turned and blew the smoke toward the window. "Hey, Silas."

"You guys gonna turn her into a pothead?" he asked with a frown and a glower.

"If that's what it takes to keep food and fluids in her," Chuck said.

"Hmm. Well, then I'm all for it. Do you think that stuff will cure my rheumatism?"

"Maybe," Papa Doc said. "But one of us better stay straight in case we have to drive somewhere."

"Good plan," Silas said. "Next time, you're the designated driver."

"Are you gonna hang onto that thing all day or let me see if I can find the ultimate cure to morning sickness?" Grace said sternly, then started giggling. "Maybe I did get some of it the first time. At least, I don't feel like I'm going to puke. Still, let's make sure."

Grace pinched the reefer with her fingers, pinkie extended, while Chuck lit it. "Watch it," he said. "I think I'd better get you a pipe. I don't want you getting burned."

"I'll let her use my bong," Papa Doc said. "It makes the smoke smoother. It's less harsh when it runs through water."

"Well, aren't you full of surprises," Silas said. "And here I thought I had you all figured out."

"Let's hope you never figure out all my secrets, Silas. Come on. Help me fix supper. I have a feeling there will be four at the dinner table tonight."

***

October 1991

"Anybody home?" Hal sang out.

"Shoot! Busted!" Grace said, then rushed to hide the bong in the closet.

Papa Doc hollered, "Be right out," then opened the window the rest of the way and clicked on the fan.

Grace picked up an aerosol can and spritzed a wide swath of rose scent. "Just a sec," she said, then giggled as she realized that both she and Papa Doc were calling from her bedroom, asking for a little more time.

Hal didn't say a word when the two walked into the living room, stifling guilty grins. He took a deep breath, then let it out slowly. *Ah, the skunk's back in the rose garden. As long as both of them can eat again, who cares what settles their stomachs or gives them an appetite?*

"We're here. What's up, Dad?"

"I have some news for you," he said, then looked around. "Where is everyone?"

"Right here," Papa Doc said, then started laughing for no apparent reason.

"You know, Doc," Hal said, shaking his head in disbelief. "I know what you two do in there. I mean, I wasn't born yesterday and I did do two tours in Vietnam."

"Huh?" Grace asked.

"He means he recognizes the smell of marijuana," Doc said. "So, is it good news? And do you want a toke to celebrate? Or is it bad news, and you want a toke to chill?"

"Neither on the smoking. Victoria can smell a fart before it comes out a gnat's ass. I don't dare even walk past the perfume counter at Nordstrom's for fear she'll accuse me of having a girlfriend who wears Chanel No. 5."

"Yup, that's Mother! So, good or bad – great or horrid – on the news?"

"It's fantastically great news! Silas worked his magic. Turns out that Victoria was so turned on by the idea of a guy coming over to give her a little personal relief that she didn't even look for a camera in the spa room. I have two angles of her getting the thousand-dollar treatment by this guy." Hal took a deep breath and stifled a blush. "Excuse me, but he really does deserve the name André the Giant."

"When are you going to file for divorce?" Grace asked.

"I'm not in any hurry now. I've got a comfortable routine. My office crew doesn't need me breathing down their necks to do a good job. Plus, coming out here a couple times a week might not be so easy if I'm loaded up with lawyers' appointments."

"Don't you want a life, Dad?"

"I do, but on my terms. But, do you want to know the real reason I'm willing to wait? Or at least a major one?"

Papa Doc and Grace nodded, then started giggling again from being high.

"This guy she's screwing charges a fortune, but she keeps calling him over! We've had separate bank accounts for years, but she isn't aware that I can watch where her money goes. I know she's pilfered from your college trust and a few other funds over the years, but I'm watching and keeping track of everything for when I file for divorce. I know exactly how much she's taken and from which accounts, and how much she has left in her personal one. And you know what? Her funds are finite. She has no way of embezzling another nickel now that I froze your accounts. I also cut off her allowance when she got mouthy beyond my tolerance. She'll be single with no job or skills to get one. Broke and stuck with a lawyer-proof prenuptial agreement.

"Oh, and to add a little spice to the pizza, I let Sally go. I gave her the option of taking a two-month vacation with a bonus or I'd help her find a new job. I just wanted her away from the house so your mother's trysts with André could continue. Not only is the upkeep of the house now your mother's responsibility, but she's almost broke. All I have to do is keep the VCRs loaded with blank tapes and multiple backups of the recorded ones in case of theft or fire. Speaking of that, I have one set of them on the porch right now."

"Well, that sounds like good news to me. The impending divorce – not the homemade porn movies," Papa Doc said. "Silas has a vault we can put them in. You might not ever need them, though. Just letting her know where the cameras are after the fact may be enough."

"Ew, my mother a potential porn star," Grace said, then giggled. "I don't think anything I can do will top that one."

"Let's hope not," Hal said. "I'm just sorry you've had such a miserable time. I certainly didn't know she was so bad. I really did do the best I could."

"You did and I knew it. Plus, you kept Sally in my life. Now all I have to do is get through this pregnancy."

Papa Doc started laughing out loud. "So, you think that all your troubles are going to end with childbirth? Sweetheart, they're just beginning."

Grace stilled suddenly, her secret choking her. *How am I going to give this child or children up for adoption with these men so eager to be grandpas? I have to get an advocate.*

Chapter 9
The Secret

December 2, 1991

"I can't take it any longer," Grace groaned. "I can't possibly get any bigger, either. Look at these stretch marks! Even with a pound a cocoa butter a day, my skin's practically ripping apart! Not to mention my boobs look like hot water bottles on top of a medicine ball."

Chuck brought out the blood pressure cuff and wrapped it around her upper arm, silently counting her rants and raves. *Eighty-four today. Not even noon and she's beat her personal best on complaints.*

"We don't use a pound of cocoa butter," he said, squeezing the bulb to inflate the cuff.

"Ouch! Do you have to make it so tight?"

"Actually, yes, I do. If we can't get your blood pressure down, you're going to have to have an emergency C-section. That means going to the hospital and loss of your anonymity. Is that what you want?"

"No," Grace said, quickly switching her rant to a pout.

"Still too high. How's your appetite? Have you eaten anything today?"

"You know everything I eat and drink. You may not weigh it out, but that calculating mind of yours catalogs everything."

Chuck bent forward and gave her a kiss on the top of the head. "You say that like it's a bad thing. Now, do you want to try walking a little?"

Taking his outstretched arm, Grace sat up as straight as she could and swung her legs over the edge of the hospital bed he had brought in for her. "Look at my feet; they're huge! I look like I have cankles, not ankles."

"Cankles?"

"My leg goes from knee to foot, the calf and ankle the same size."

"Well," Chuck said, still trying to switch up her grumbling, "at least you have a matched pair."

Grace's face squeezed into an exaggerated pout that burst into a full laugh when she looked up and saw him waiting for her reaction. "How do you do that? I mean, I'm so emotionally pissed and physically miserable, and you can still make me laugh."

"You're worth it, Grace. Don't let anyone ever tell you differently. You are, and always will be, my best friend. You have to know that."

"I do," she said, then let him help her to a standing position. "So, does that mean I can share my inner fears and hopes and stupid ideas with you without being judged?"

"Yup. Now watch the threshold. We're not going outside, but I want to see how well you can ride in a vehicle. Just in case."

"There's no way I'm going anywhere in that ground-hugging Ferrari of Papa Doc's."

Chuck swung the door open completely and let her take it in. "An ambulance? Where in the hell did that come from?"

"The ambulance stork delivered it last night," he said drolly, grinning.

"Do you really want me to get in it?" she asked, suddenly fearful.

"No, I just wanted to let you know that if we can't get you to calm down and stop being so angry at the world, this is what you'll be riding in to the hospital. The babies will certainly be too small to survive on their own. They'll be in incubators with tubes stuck down their throats, cotton pads over their eyes, little shunts in their veins…"

"Stop it!" Grace whispered harshly. "I get it. I mean, bringing an ambulance home is a little overkill, don't you think?"

"How many times have I told you to take a chill pill? You said you didn't want to smoke anymore because you wanted to embrace your rage. Let. It. Go! Life sucks sometimes. Other times, like this, what you see as a hardship is just a stretch of your life that it's hard to get through. You have support, though. Between me and the three grandpas, that's four people who'd do anything in the world for you. Do you know how rare that it?"

"But my babies don't have a father…"

"I hear your words, but what I understand is that you're saying you don't have a husband. I've told you dozens of times, we can get married."

"Chuck, I love you, I really do, but you and I both know that you may be plumbed like a man who'd be a great husband, but you're not wired the right way. I mean…"

"Yes, I know what you mean," Chuck said. "I'm queer."

"Don't say that like you're ashamed of it. I really do wish you'd come out of the closet. It's not as if it's wrong. So, you're like a minority of the human population, not the majority. Only cruel people have decided that there's something wrong with it, okay?"

Chuck looked at her and shook his head in awe. "How can you be straight and have such a profound insight on life and still be only eighteen years old?"

"I'm either blessed or cursed. Take your pick."

"Kind of like me?"

Grace's shoulders slumped as she realized they had so much in common despite age, background, and current physical condition. "Okay, my 'oh so not identical twin,' you've helped me with everything else so far, I want to ask one more favor. And it's a biggie."

"Anything for you," Chuck said aloud, hoping she didn't hear the '*Ah, shit! What now?*' gut response he had stifled.

Grace shut her eyes and paused. How could she ask? She imagined the words written on a blackboard in chalk and read them aloud, "I want you to take the babies and give them up for adoption."

"Whoa! Wait! What? Huh?" Chuck sputtered. "I mean, you

don't want your own children?"

"Not now. Not with the way my life is."

"Oh, no, no, no. You can't just say, 'I don't want you because it's not convenient. I'll come back for you when I get my head on straight.'"

"You don't understand…"

"Oh, yes I do understand," Chuck said, his hands on her cheeks, forcing her to look him in the eye. "You are under the influence of a double dose of pregnancy hormones. You want out of this situation completely, to walk away from everything and get your perky little figure back so you can hit the road and find your long-lost Dusty. Well, I've got news for you. It isn't that easy. This isn't playable with the hand you've been dealt. These two babies will be loved and cherished beyond what ninety-nine percent of two-parent families can provide."

"My mother will find a way to mess this up, no matter how careful you and the others have been. I feel it in my bones. I have to protect these little guys or gals. I'm not asking you to help me give them away because I don't love them. It's just the opposite. I'm doing it because I *do* love them. Please, I can't reach out and find the right parents with Papa Doc, Silas, and my dad watching me. You're sharp and have excellent taste. I have one request. I'd prefer a family from a lower-income bracket unless it's a stellar man, woman, or couple who want to adopt, and then I don't care. At least poor folks love each other for who they are, not what they have or will inherit."

"You sound like you've been planning this for a while. Any other restrictions?"

"Other than the obvious: don't let my mother know anything about me having twins."

"So, since you've thought this whole thing out, how are we going to hide it from the men?"

"When the time comes, take me away, deliver them, and tell the guys that the babies died. I'll be distraught no matter what. I'm sure you will be, too. We won't have to fake anything."

"You're not leaving me much time for this. You know your blood pressure is sky-high. You shouldn't even be at home."

"If I was in a hospital, what would you be doing for me?"

"I told you. I'd take the babies early and hope for the best for them, all while trying to save your life."

"What? You mean my life's in danger?" Grace asked, stumbling toward the special lift recliner her father had bought for her.

"Isn't that what I've been telling you?"

"No, it isn't. So, if you want me to stop stressing, the first thing you have to do is take away my reason: the future of these twins. Promise me right now you'll find homes for these two and not let the men know about it."

"You know, for not being intimate, you sure have my balls in a vice…"

"Promise me or there's no way I can stop stressing."

"And you're turning the handle, ready to emasculate me."

"I'll let up. All you have to do is say the word."

"All right. I promise you I will find homes for your two babies and will not tell anyone about them."

"Anyone, especially our dads and Silas," Grace prompted.

"I promise. Cross my heart, hope to die, pinky swear and all that. Geez, Grace. Isn't my word enough?"

"Yes, it is. I just wanted to watch you squirm."

"Yeah, well, when it's delivery time, I'll get my payback. I've only delivered twins once. I have to tell you, the mother looked most uncomfortable."

"I'm sure you're understating the event. If it's at all possible, knock me out."

Ring! Ring! Ring!

"Saved by the bell. Let me answer that. Don't run away," Chuck said.

Grace put a hand on each arm of the recliner as if to get up, then changed her mind and settled back into the chair. "Couldn't even if I wanted."

"Hello. She what? Oh, tell me you're pulling my leg. How close is she? How did she find out? No, I didn't tell a soul, either. Okay. I'll go to plan B. I don't want to say it in case this line is tapped. Hey, I gotta scoot. Oh, and thanks in advance. Bye."

"Who was that?" Grace asked, her finger now pressing the chair lift button, rising up.

Chuck ran his fingers through his hair, exasperated and confused, not knowing what to do first. He looked over at her. "Yes, get up. Shoot, you don't even have time to change clothes. I'll grab the keys and your bag while you make your way to the garage. I'll help you get in the ambulance. You can ride in the front, can't you? I don't want you in the back alone."

"You're babbling, but that means the shit has hit the fan. Yes, I'd rather ride in front."

Chuck snatched his keys from the rack in the kitchen, dashed into Grace's room and grabbed her overnight bag, and was at the pantry door to the garage by the time she had reached it. "Watch your step."

"Are you going to tell me what's going on?"

"Not until we're on the road."

"Crap. That means my mother found out, right?"

"I wish you weren't so perceptive sometimes. Yes, but we have it under control. Come on, let's go. I don't know how much time we have."

He opened the passenger door of the ambulance, threw the overnight bag behind the seats, scooted the seat back a couple more notches, then offered her a hand up. After trying three times to hoist herself up with the grab bar, she admitted defeat and asked, "Help, please."

Chuck boosted her fanny up and over, into the seat. "Seatbelt," he said, offering the extended buckle to the now breathless woman. She tucked the nylon strap under her belly, then leaned back and tried to catch her breath. Chuck ran around the ambulance and jumped in, his nervous energy practically radiating as sparks.

Grace bit at the cuticle of her fingernail as Chuck strummed on the steering wheel, both anxious for the garage door to hurry up and open. As soon as there was clearance for the rooftop beacons, Chuck stomped the accelerator. Backing off the gas, he carefully negotiated the curves of the long icy driveway, slowing to a crawl at the bottom of the hill, looking for other vehicles. There weren't any. Victoria wasn't around. He stopped ten feet before the gatehouse and put the ambulance in park.

Grace started to chew on her finger again, thought better of it, and tried to put her hand under her armpit. When the seat belt got in her way, she settled on interlacing her fingers and resting them on her belly. "Damn! Why did you stop? And where did you say we're going?"

"The first thing I want to do is see what happened to the guard."

"Wait. You mean my mother's not here? I thought that's why we were hightailing it out of here."

"Dad's security team has a truck they use. Can you see *any* vehicles around here, because I can't?"

Grace twisted in her seat and looked out her side window. "Nope. Nothing here. Maybe the guard went out for a pizza or something."

Suddenly, a light flipped on inside the gatehouse and a broad-shouldered man with dark curly hair pulled back in a queue stepped outside. Grace didn't know who the usual guard was, but the uniform this man was wearing was at least two sizes too small, the few buttons that were fastened, strained.

"Good evening, sir," he said. He paused then looked through the driver's window, squinting past Chuck to check out Grace.

Chuck leaned forward, doing his best to block the man's view. "What happened to Caleb? I thought he was working tonight."

"Who? Oh, Caleb?" the replacement guard said to Chuck with a slight French accent. "Yes, he had a stomach pain and chose to leave. The agency sent me over," he explained, then looked behind Chuck to check out Grace again.

Chuck took his foot off the brake, driving forward slowly as he spoke. "No worries," he said, denying the guard the chance of seeing more of Grace than he already had.

"Let me guess. That wasn't the regular guy and you smelled a rat?" Grace asked as they pulled away.

"Worse," Chuck growled as he drove onto the access road to the highway. "That was André."

"Who's André? Oh, wait. You mean the man my mother was having sex with? How do you know what he looks like?"

Chuck glanced over at her – grimaced but didn't say a word – then returned to watching the road.

"Chuck?"

"Okay. I was curious. I skimmed through one of the videos before I locked them away."

Grace giggled. "Well, he can't have been that impressive if you know what his face looks like…"

Chuck's somber face of embarrassment cracked and three seconds later, he was laughing along with her. "So, it looks like the best hung Canadian in town may have caught a glimpse of your pregnant body. I doubt that he took a second job as a guard, especially if he's making as much per session as your dad says he is. I'd say Victoria's either conned him into getting blackmail information on you or he was here to try to kidnap you. Since the regular guards are nowhere to be seen, I'd say he either bribed someone to stay away or he has the regular guy tied up somewhere."

"I sure hope it isn't worse than that. You don't think he'd kill anyone, do you?"

"I doubt it, but then again, I tend to think the best about everyone. I'm PollyAndy, remember?"

"Well, since my dad said he cut my mother off, I wouldn't put it past her to have taken out a life insurance policy or two on me with her as beneficiary…"

Chuck reached over reflexively to protect her, one hand on the steering wheel, the other on her left arm that was resting across her belly. "You don't think she'd really do that, do you?"

"Chuck, you didn't see the way she looked at me when she was fingering that wine bottle, ready to rape me with it and blame it on my boyfriend. I don't think she cares about anyone other than herself."

"We have to get you out of this town. Time for Plan C. Sorry, but we're going to have to let our guys worry for a while. We may have a mole or rat or someone's wiretapped the house. Right now, it's just you and me, kid."

Grace glanced at her side mirror again, noticing the distinctive headlights getting closer and closer. "Not exactly. I think there's a Jaguar on our tail. I'm sure there's more than one in the area, but this one's a classic."

"Your mother's?" Chuck asked, checking his mirror to verify.

"Yup. How many people do you think would tailgate an ambulance?"

"Hold on, Grace," Chuck said, reaching up to flip on the siren and rotating beacon. "It's time to clear the roads ahead and hope your mother can't corner worth a damn without studded tires."

Grace reached out and grabbed the door and his armrest. "Let's go, Mario!"

Chapter 10
The Shootout

"Crap!" Chuck steered into the spin, but the heavy, awkward, and boxy vehicle still wound up slipping off the road, pointed in the wrong direction.

"Is she still following us?" Grace asked.

"I don't know. I lost track of her. If she is, she has her headlights off." He put his hand on the door handle, ready to open it. "Wait here. I want to see if I have enough room to turn around and get us out of here."

"Be careful," Grace said.

"Always."

Using a flashlight, Chuck looked under the ambulance and saw that he hadn't high-centered it. He could put it in reverse and – if he got enough traction – get back onto the road, make a three-point turn, and be pointed in the right direction in less than a minute. If he hadn't looked first and just driven forward, he would have been stuck. A screwed sitting duck. "Glad I trusted my instincts and checked."

Crunch! Crunch!

Chuck switched off the flashlight and froze at the sound of the icy ground breaking apart under approaching footsteps.

Pop! Pop!

He dropped to the pavement, away from the silenced gunshots, his back pressed close to the ambulance.

Click! Slam! Thunk, rumble. Omph!

"Get in and drive!" Gracie shouted to him from her window.

Chuck sprang to his feet and jumped in, ready to stomp on the gas, then remembered to back up first or be stuck. He grunted as he turned the steering wheel hard, making do with a two-point turn, back onto the road with an emotionally charged and frantic getaway. He watched the side mirror as he sped away. The stunned thin person on the ground rose slowly, waving a fist in rage, any words absorbed by the crackle of studded tires and road noise as he sped away.

"Who or what just happened?" he asked.

"That was my mother. She fired two shots into the window, so I slam-opened the door and knocked her ass down."

"What?" Chuck leaned forward and looked over at her but the dashboard lights were too dim for him to see if any damage had been done. "I can't see. Did she hit you? How bad?"

Grace kept a tight grip on her right upper arm with her left hand. "Yes, she hit me, but I don't know how bad it is. I'm afraid to look. I'm sure I'll live but it hurts like hell."

"Here, put pressure on it with this." Chuck grabbed the sweatshirt hanging behind him and tossed it to her. "And if it hurts, that's a good thing. The ones you don't feel are the really bad ones."

Grace adjusted the bulky sweatshirt so it was against the two holes in the window, blocking the freezing air and also pressing against her wound or wounds. "Okay. I got this. So, to distract me, please tell me what Plan C is. And keep talking."

"I'm going to take you to a friend I met in an online chat room. That's an internet thing if you don't already know."

"So, have you met him in person before. I assume it's a guy and not a girl."

"Yes, he's a guy; you're the only girl in my life. We've kicked it up a couple notches, exchanging real names and pictures. I checked him out thoroughly. Actually, I've talked to him on the phone a few times, too. As in, I called his office and asked to speak with him, using my Chat Room username the first time. He's a decent guy, has a practice in New Hampshire, and most importantly, he's discreet."

"Pardon my naivety, but what does that mean? Is it a gay thing?"

"We're both still in the closet, but that's not what I mean. It means he can treat your bullet wound and not report it to the authorities."

“You mean, my mother is going to get away with shooting me?” Grace asked, her voice ending on a high note of frustration.

“Do you want to go to the police and press charges? You do know that you and your huge pregnant belly would be thrown into the spotlight immediately, right? Everyone would want to know what’s been going on in the life of Victoria Stillwell’s missing daughter. Being an unwed mother may or may not make a difference to many but having a wife who shot his daughter might just mess up your father’s business big time.”

“Okay. Let’s keep him out of this for now. Besides, if it’s known I’m pregnant, I’ll pretty much have to keep the babies. I’m still positive that they’d have a better life away from me. Even more so now that their grandmother is a felon, that she tried to murder her own daughter. The twins would never live down that stigma.”

Grace shuddered, then realized it wasn’t just the emotions causing a chill. “Can you turn up the heater? I’m cold.”

“It’s like a hundred degrees in here… Oh, crap. How much blood have you lost?”

“How in the hell should I know? It’s not as if I have a meter running on this thing. Shit! I can’t even see it.”

Chuck reached over, ready to turn on the lights, then stopped at her screech. “Don’t! What difference does it make? We’re going wherever we’re going as fast as possible, right? One or both of us is going to freak out if I’ve lost too much blood. We can’t do anything about it anyhow unless you have a pint of blood in the back and can pump it into me and drive at the same time.”

“Grace, sometimes your logic amazes me. Just chill and leave getting there to me. At least, we don’t have a tail anymore,” Chuck said, quickly glancing into the side mirror to confirm.

“I just hope the door broke her nose and blacked an eye or two. So much for honoring my mother.”

“Well, look on the bright side: at least you still have one good parent left.”

“All right, PollyAndy. Let’s pass the time talking about

something else. Tell me about your cyber lover."

Chuck sighed in resignation. He'd share anything with her to keep her mind off her dilemma. They had over a hundred miles ahead of them, and a winter storm was coming in. It was going to be a long night.

***

Chuck looked over and saw the conversation had stopped because Grace had fallen asleep in mid-sentence. He reached over and touched her cheek. Warm and dry, her breathing regular. According to the road signs and odometer, he only had twenty miles to go. He pulled the cellphone out of his front pocket, flipped it open, and started punching numbers.

"Hello? Buddy? Yeah, this is Chuck. I know, we were due for a chat an hour ago but life suddenly got complicated. I'm on the road with a very pregnant and gun-shot woman. Yes, it's Grace. Her crazy mother fired at her twice, and at least one bullet caught her in the arm. Can I come to your clinic? Yes, your in-home clinic would definitely be better. I'm driving an ambulance, so I'll be easy to spot coming in. Just tell me whether I should come in with lights, siren, or silent. Okay, silent it is. Duh! Especially if we're going to your house. Do you have a garage this beast will fit in? I don't want it spotted on the road. No, it's legal – bought and paid for. I'm pretty sure no one's following me or even knows my destination. Nope. Only you and I know where we'll be. She already signed the affidavit for the adoptions, but we didn't have a witness. I'd rather start from scratch with one signed in New Hampshire. Sort of wish you were a notary, too. You are? Aren't you a bundle of surprises? Yeah, we'll find out more about those surprises later. We need to take care of her before we get to know each other better *that* way. All right. See you soon. *Ciao!"*

The hypnotic drone of studded tires on asphalt and the gentle swaying of dips and curves disappeared suddenly as the ambulance slowed to a stop at the traffic light,
waking up Grace.

"Hey, there, sleepyhead. How ya' doing?"

Grace blinked and looked around to see where she was, trying to orient herself. *Chuck. Okay, but why are we in a car? Why do these traffic lights and buildings look different?* "Where are we?"

"Someplace safe. How's your arm?"

Pulling herself upright, Grace squeaked in pain. "Ouch! What? Wait just a sec. It's coming back to me…shot in the arm by my own mother. Damn! Where's one of your dad's brownies when I need one?"

"I packed lots of your special comfort food and smokes for you, so don't worry. But we'll have to wait a few minutes." Chuck picked up the map from the center console and flipped on the light, verified his location, then went dark again. "Two more blocks to go and we're safe. Buddy's a doctor, too. Actually, he's an obstetrician. Now, before we get there, are you still certain you want to give these two babies up for adoption?"

"Why do you keep asking me? Yes, I'm certain. I already signed those papers you drew up. I want them safe, out of the spotlight, and in a nice boring community, away from Mother."

"The only reason I ask is because we never had those papers notarized. I can print up another set and have Buddy notarize them. He has several good couples looking to adopt. You can even interview them if you want."

"No. I'd prefer it if you would do that part. That is if you don't mind. Damn. You've already cleared half your workdays and all of your weekends for me. Are you going to stay here with me until I deliver, or are you just dumping me on this Dr. Buddy?"

"I'm not dumping you. This is sudden, though. I may have to get an imaginary exotic and highly contagious disease to explain my absence."

"I'm sure you can think of something. Plus, that would be a good reason for you to stay away from our dads and Silas, too. And as far as my disappearance, why don't you just leave it alone? If the cops start snooping, they'll figure out my mother and André are involved and bust them for kidnapping. I wouldn't put it past her to have already sent a ransom note to my dad."

"You know, you're pretty smart for only eighteen."

"I read a lot of mystery novels."

"Well, your life would be a good one, at least the last seven months. Hey, look up ahead!"

Grace saw a beautiful house directly ahead, the garage door opening at 3 AM, apparently for them. "Is this the place?"

"I think so," Chuck said, leaning forward to catch a glimpse of the address on the gatepost. "Yup. We're home. At least, home for the next month or so."

Grace sighed and leaned back into the seat. "God, I hope time flies. I am so ready for all this to be over."

Chuck pulled into the driveway, not commenting aloud on her remark. *Me, too, Gracie. Me, too.*

A tall dark-skinned man with slicked-back hair in navy blue pajamas pointed the way to the designated parking spot in the large subterranean garage. The stranger waited on the passenger side of the ambulance as Chuck pulled in, his hand raised in a fist to indicate stop. Smiling and nodding a quick silent greeting, he opened the door for Grace. Instinctively, the medic held fast the bloodied sweatshirt being used as a bandage. Ignoring the perfunctory medical attention he had just provided her, he said, "Greetings. You must be Grace."

"That's me," she answered. Grace reached for the dash, using her good hand to help pivot her in the seat, ready to get out.

"Please allow me to assist. I'm sure it's been a long ride." Hand out, ready to help her stand, he said, "Your legs may not be ready for your weight."

Grace stumbled as she exited the vehicle, embarrassed both that he had been right and that he had to catch her to keep her from falling. "What a first impression," she grumbled, then straightened up. "You must be Buddy."

Buddy put his arm around her back and under her arm. "My full name is Guamtam Deepak Jeet, but yes, please call me Buddy." He looked up and saw Chuck watching them. "And you must be Chuck."

"Charles Darwin Armstrong, but if you call for Charles, I'll think I'm in trouble and won't answer."

"All right, Chuck. If you would, just inside that door, you'll find a wheelchair. It might be easier on the lady if she rides."

"I'm no lady. I mean, I'd prefer it if you called me Grace. I'd rather walk, but I'm afraid my legs don't agree." She suddenly reached around and clutched at a back spasm, grunting with the unexpected pain. "Back's a deal-breaker. Bring out the wheelchair."

"You must let us take care of you," Buddy said, resisting the urge to give her a hug. "You are a special, strong lady and we want to help you. I will call you Grace, though."

"Not for long, though. I mean, no offense, but I hope we're done once this baby thing is over and I'm back…"

Grace sat down hard in the wheelchair, not bothering to finish her sentence. Where was she going after this was over? She had no life now. She still had her father, but how long would she be able to continue to lie about the twins and where they had disappeared to? He'd be heartbroken beyond repair.

"Chuck, can I have a brownie or two?" she asked, then twinged with a fake back spasm. "I'm hurting pretty bad here."

Buddy looked up at Chuck, curious about what she was asking about.

"Let's get you checked out first," Chuck said. "It appears you only have a flesh wound on your arm, but I want to look over everything. It's been a long journey in more than one way."

***

December 5, 1991

"Are you sure this is the best place to meet her?" Hal asked Silas.

"A public place, lots of witnesses, plus she's less likely to run you over with a truck inside a building."

“We both know she’s desperate, Silas, but I don’t think she’d ever lower herself to drive a work vehicle.”

“Besides the fact that she’d have to step *up* to get in a truck, from what Grace told me, she’s more of an intimidation expert who likes to throw sneaky punches. Too bad I can’t frisk her before she sits down. Let’s just hope she’s not desperate enough to shoot you for a life insurance policy.”

“Grace is my beneficiary, not her,” Hal said, sipping his coffee, his eyes still focused on the front door.

“That doesn’t mean she didn’t take out a new policy on you. She could do that as your wife.”

Hal turned back and looked at him, wide-eyed.

“Hey, just saying…”

Ding! Ding!

The brass bell on the diner door announced another person coming in. Or two. Victoria had arrived, swathed in a dark blue scarf, sporting oversized sunglasses. André was at her back, holding the door open for her. “Thank you, dear,” she said, looking up to the exotic bodybuilder and smiling with feigned sincerity.

She glanced around the room, spotted Hal and Silas in the corner, then sauntered over to their table, leaving André at the door. After waiting a moment for the men to stand up and acknowledge her or offer a seat, she pulled a chair out for herself and sat down gingerly.

The first thing Hal noticed was her nose. It wasn’t the sunglasses that made it look so big, it really was swollen and was painted with a thick coat of foundation. “What happened?” he asked, then chuckled. “Get too close to a mirror?”

“I’m here about our daughter, Grace,” she said haughtily, totally ignoring his comment.

“Since we only have one daughter, I would assume it’s Grace. So, what did you do to her? Where is she?”

Silas noticed Victoria flinch when Hal asked what she had done to Grace, then blanch in confusion at where she was. Apparently, she had done something to her but didn't know where she was. *Keep up the interrogation, Hal. You're doing great.*

"I know Grace is pregnant. Very pregnant. She needs to see a doctor. I made a few calls and my gynecologist can clear his afternoon to see her today." Victoria babbled her practiced spiel, then paused. Her whole face – save her heavily-painted nose – reddened in embarrassment as she realized what Hal had said. *Where is she? She didn't come home? He doesn't know anything... I've just been given a blank check! He thinks I have her!*

"Isn't anyone going to offer me coffee?" she asked, looking for a waitress, avoiding the truth-seeking stares of Hal and Silas.

Silas took the setting from an empty table, then walked behind the counter and grabbed a full pot of coffee. He set the cup and saucer down with a clatter, then splashed the hot black liquid into it, intentionally overfilling the cup and making a mess. "Better?" he snarled.

Victoria looked up at him with disdain, then down at the cup. She huffed and decided to ignore his rude acquiescence and continue. His impromptu dramatic production had given her enough time to devise a plan. "If you'd like to see our daughter again, you'll transfer five million dollars into my personal account. I know you have the routing numbers. You've been watching it for years," she said, ending her demand with a slight nervous twitch of her upper lip.

Hal sprung up with rage, knocking the table toward her, the cup of coffee spilling into her lap, causing her to jump, too. He grabbed her by the throat. "Where is she? What did you do to her?" he repeated, this time at full volume, spittle flying from his mouth in uncontrolled rage.

André rushed to her defense, but Silas stepped in front of him. He wasn't as tall or beefy as the wannabe pornstar boyfriend – and was twice as old – but he had more experience as a bodyguard and it showed. "Don't!" he commanded, chin out in defiance.

The frightened lover took a step back, hands dropping to his sides in defeat. He'd attached himself to another nut. Defeated and frustrated, he shook his head at the woman who had both run out of money and plans to get more. Time to shut the book on this one.

Ding! Ding!

Hal loosened his grip, brought back to his senses by the sound of the doorbell. He looked away from the terrorized Victoria and saw André leaving, his head still shaking back and forth in disgust. "Looks like someone else is fed up with your lies," Hal said. "You'll be hearing from my lawyer very soon. He's 'cleared his afternoon' for me," he added snidely.

"And that's a cut!" Silas said suddenly and dramatically. He looked around the room as if making sure everything was in place, saluting the non-existent hidden cameras. "Thank you, ladies and gentlemen. You've just participated in a scene from The Plymouth Chronicles. Watch for it in a theater near you the summer of '92."

Hal walked over to the waitress, wearing a grin of embarrassment. "Here," he said, pressing three hundred-dollar bills into her hand. "I don't think anything more than a cup or saucer was broken, but we did make a mess. Don't worry. We won't be back."

She looked down at the money, spreading the bills apart to count them. "Come back any time!" she said enthusiastically. "And she really did seem like a bitch. Hope all goes well with the divorce. Oh, and that you find your daughter…"

"Yeah, me, too," Hal said. "Me, too."

"What now?" Silas asked once they were out of the café.

"All we can do is hope that Chuck calls in. I really did think that Grace was kidnapped after you found the gatekeeper tied up. Oh, and great call on making my attack on Victoria look like a scene from a movie. That was an Oscar-worthy performance."

"Yeah, well one thing bothers me – other than where in the hell did Chuck and Grace disappear to and why – is how did Victoria get a broken nose? Lord, I hope Grace did it," Silas said, opening his car door.

"That would be nice, wouldn't it?" Hal looked at his watch. "I have time to drop in on my lawyer. I'll meet you at the compound for dinner. Should I bring fish, beef, or salad?"

"I'll pick up some crab. You go ahead and grab salad makings. I'm pretty sure there are enough steaks in the freezer for everyone if we want to get that crazy. No telling when Doc's coming home. He's making a personal appearance at Chuck's downtown clinic. Lots of folks remember him from way back when. If Chuck left a clue to where he went, Papa Doc will sniff it out."

"Yeah, well, according to him, he learned from the best. See you at supper."

***

Papa Doc pulled up to the gate and rolled down the window. "How's the head?" he asked the guard.

"I still have a headache, but the embarrassment is the worst part. I've been working here for ten years, Doctor Armstrong, and never a lick of trouble. Then one woman comes in and blindsides me."

"Don't worry about it. I'm just glad it wasn't something more serious. Let me know if you see either Victoria or that boyfriend of hers snooping around. Don't engage them; just call me immediately and we'll go from there. Oh, and anything on my number three son?"

"No, sir. I haven't heard from or seen him in about a week."

"All right. I'm in for the evening," Papa Doc said, then drove up to the house, frustrated, defeated, but still hopeful.

As soon as he walked in the door, Silas looked up, suddenly crestfallen that Doc was alone. "So, I guess it's just three old bachelors for dinner? Anyhow, what did you find out downtown?"

"Chuck sent a fax in from a restricted phone number. 'We've been exposed to Ebola virus. Must stay isolated to protect all. Chuck.'" Papa Doc crumpled up the copy of the fax and tossed it into the trash.

"Hey, maybe there's a clue or two on there," Silas said.

"Already found it. Chuck's saying, 'Leave us alone for a while. We have some crap we have to work through.' Damn. I know he cares a lot for that woman, even if he is gay. Still, he's taking her away from her father," Doc said, looking at Hal.

"I've seen those two together," Hal said. "He's doing it because she wants him to, not the other way around. All we can do is be patient. If we stir up crap, this place will be a feeding frenzy for the press. Keep on keeping on so the roads remain clear and unwatched, ready for them when they decide to come home."

"Them and the babies," Papa Doc said hopefully.

Hal and Silas looked at each other and winced. Either Doc hadn't noticed that Grace hadn't ordered one piece of baby clothing or furniture, or he was choosing to ignore that glaring fact. Either way, neither of them would bring it up.

Chapter 11
Oblivion

December 3, 1991

"Not much needed for that," Chuck said, sealing the gauze on Grace's upper arm with adhesive tape. "You were lucky."

"Will it scar?"

"Probably," Chuck said, "but you can say you walked into a sharp branch or fell on a piece of pipe if you don't want bragging rights about being shot at close range by a crazy woman." He kissed her on top of the head. "Now, how is everything else?"

"I hurt everywhere. I feel like I'm a gray whale trapped in a harbor seal's body: bloated and ugly and ready to pop out of my skin no matter what." Grace looked over at Buddy, waiting silently on a stool in the corner. She knew he was letting Chuck take care of her injury before intruding on her emotionally delicate situation. Both men were handsome, gentle, and considerate: no wonder they were attracted to each other.

"Buddy, do you want to check me out so you two can have some time getting acquainted? I'm sure you have a place for me to sleep when you're done. Or at least, try to sleep. I can't find a comfortable position these days, but I'm still willing to look for one."

"Yes, I have a room. How about you lie back, so I can listen to those three heartbeats."

"Three?" Grace squealed.

Chuck, standing behind Grace and out of her line of sight, frowned at Buddy. "Three," Buddy clarified with a nervous smile. "The two babies and yours."

"Oh, yeah. I guess I wasn't thinking of it like that."

"Can I check her BP for you?" Chuck asked, trying not to flirt but still remain helpful and close at the same time.

"Yes, please," Buddy said. "May I?" he asked Grace, his hand on the hem of her maternity shirt.

"Go for it," she said, then tried to relax into the examination table. "Chuck said twins usually come early. Please tell me he's right? I don't want to wait six more weeks."

"Usually two weeks early is fine. As long as the babies are around five pounds each, they should be healthy enough to live outside of the mother. The lungs are usually developed by then."

"Four more weeks to go?"

"Yes, but I can make your wait much more comfortable. Hold still a moment and let me listen to heartbeats. Then I have a surprise for you; one you will be very happy with."

Buddy traversed her belly with hands and stethoscope, verifying the babies' body positions so he could find their heartbeats. He tried to keep his face stoic, but when he heard the third strong and rapid fetal heart, he allowed a smile to escape. "One more," he said, then offered her his hand to help her sit up. "Breathe normally," and checked her lungs, too.

"Perfect." He looked at Chuck. "Her blood pressure?" he asked.

Chuck grimaced slightly. "Too high. I don't like it, but after what she's just been through, I think anyone would have those kinds of numbers."

"Come with me, Grace. It's time for your surprise." Buddy helped her get off the examination table and back into the wheelchair.

"Now you really got me going," Chuck said as he followed them down the hall.

"What? You don't know where we're going?" Grace asked, frightened all over again.

"No, but I trust him, and you should, too," Chuck said, patting her shoulder in reassurance.

"What do I have to lose?" Grace relaxed back into the wheelchair, then grumbled, "I have nothing."

When they came to a stop outside a room with an industrial-sized door, Chuck squatted down beside her. "You will always have me. Always, or as long as you want me in your life."

Grace quickly looked over at Buddy, avoiding eye contact with Chuck's new beau apparent, letting Chuck know that she was referring to his new friend.

"I can love more than one person at a time. I just won't be sleeping with both of you," he whispered.

"You can sleep with him as long as you leave me with Alice P."

"Alice B.," he corrected. "Yes, I'll make sure you're well-stocked with sweets and smokes of oblivion."

"Right in here," Buddy said, opening the door to the inner room. "It's an immersion tank, filled with magnesium sulfate."

"Huh?" Grace asked, pulling back, trying to move away from the tomb-like enclosure.

"Wow. I like it," Chuck said, then explained it to Grace. "It's a giant Epsom salts bath. You won't feel the weight or pressure of the pregnancy while you're in there. Plus, your body is probably deficient in magnesium. That might be another reason you hurt all the time. This will help take care of that. And if you're not hurting, your blood pressure should come down. Win-win-win situation."

"Can I use the bathroom before I go in? And I guess you two don't care that I don't have a bathing suit, do you? I mean, you're both gay, right?"

"Aye," Chuck said, "we're both fairies. But more importantly, we're both doctors. The only way we're interested in your body is to make sure you stay healthy and keep those babies inside of you long enough that they can survive in the outside world. Any other concerns?"

"Minute by minute," Grace said. "Potty break then a bath. After that, maybe a bite to eat and a warm place to sleep. What more could anyone ask?"

"A healthy delivery and a new life for you. Silas is still searching for Dusty. I know we never talk about it so we don't stress you. I just want to make sure you know that he's still searching."

"Thanks. I needed that."

***

Knock! Knock!

"Come in."

"How'd you sleep?" Buddy asked, balancing the breakfast tray one-handed as he opened the door.

"I can't believe I slept so long. I'll bet I was out for three hours straight at least once. If I didn't have to get up to pee so much, I would have slept straight through. Still, if this clock is right, I've been out of it for twelve hours!"

"The clock is right. Chuck said you didn't care for coffee, but I thought you might like some herbal tea. Normally, I'd advocate exercise, but I'd rather you rest every chance you get. Only get up for bathroom breaks. You can ring that bell and someone will come and take you via wheelchair to the float tank or into the library to choose a book or videotape. No walking beyond the bathroom. Oh," Buddy held out a colorful cotton thong with a pendant on it. "Press this if you fall and can't reach the bell."

"Where's Chuck?"

"He said he had an errand to run."

Grace lifted an eyebrow in doubt and shook her head. "If we're all going to get along for the next month or so, you'd better tell me the whole truth."

"He wanted to have that paper we all signed last night filed as soon as possible."

"I'm not going to change my mind," Grace said.

"Even if your Dusty shows up?" Buddy asked, using the same raised-eyebrow gesture.

"Do you think he's going to want this blimp of a body?"

"Grace, men love the person, in here," he thumped his chest, "not the fabric-wrapped flesh container. Now, I might be ruining the prospects of two couples getting a child by speaking with you like this, but I don't want you to have regrets."

"Did Chuck put you up to this? Is he standing outside, waiting to hear me recant so he can tear up the release of parental rights, then take the babies back to our fathers to raise as one giant dysfunctional family?"

"Eat. Please. You have low blood sugar. If you can't do it for yourself, do it for the people who are going to take these babies home next month. If you don't keep your 'flesh container' healthy, all this will have been for nothing. We'll be burying little corpses, then sending you on your way a few weeks sooner. Is that what you want?"

Grace glowered at him, angry that he had gotten through her thick skin, then grabbed a piece of toast and stuffed it in her mouth rather than answer his question. "Go away," she said with cheeks full. "I have some babies to build."

Buddy closed the door behind him, then let a smile escape. The chances of the babies surviving just went up.

Chapter 12
Shopping

Late December 1991
The Mall of New Hampshire

Chuck pulled into the mega-mall's parking lot driving his new old ride: an all-wheel-drive van. It was boxy but discreet, an electrician's work vehicle that had been converted into a mini-home on wheels. It had a bed, cabinets, propane stove and refrigerator. It didn't have a bathroom but did have a battery-powered water pump and basin for quick clean-ups. The seller assured him that a five-gallon bucket with trash bag liners would work for any long stretches between gas station pit stops. The young man was more than happy to make a swap for the ambulance – an exotic and hard-to-find vehicle. He had given Chuck his full asking price, plus marked down the trade-in value of his van because it needed a paint job. Both buyer and seller walked away happy with the transaction.

"A low-profile ride and enough cash in my pocket to outfit my cross-country motorhome with a nursery and supplies for at least a month. No need to use that trackable, traceable credit card yet. The stars are aligning, Chuck. You're doing great."

The mall seemed to be even larger on the inside than it was on the outside. He looked for a mall directory, couldn't find one, so walked into the biggest store on his end of the building. "Excuse me, but do you know where I can find clothing for preemies?"

The bleached blonde at the jewelry counter looked Chuck up and down like he was an idiot, batting her long fake eyelashes at him as if shooing him away. "We don't have that in this store, sir," she replied haughtily.

Chuck started to explain that he just wanted to know if there even was such a store in the mall or where a directory was so he could figure it out himself, then realized that if it didn't pertain to her or her commission, she probably didn't want to hear about it.

Suddenly, he felt a soft hand on his elbow, trying to get his attention. "I know where one is, and I'm going that way." The friendly lady in a sporty mauve business suit was all smiles at the prospect of helping him, proving that classy clothes and good grooming didn't make a snob. "Care to join me?"

"Yes, I'd like that. My name's Chuck and I'm new in town," he explained as they walked down the corridor. "I have no idea where to shop. I'm looking for items for a premature little girl."

"How much did she weigh?" asked the woman, stopping suddenly, her hand grasping his upper arm.

Momentarily stunned by her intense reaction, Chuck quickly realized that she was genuinely interested, eager to hear any information or hints about tiny baby girls. "She hasn't been born yet," he said, "but I know she'll be under term weight."

"Same here," she replied, then pulled him along with a renewed excitement. "I'm Gloria Thornwhistle, by the way. I'm getting a daughter in one week, maybe sooner. We couldn't conceive so decided to adopt. We just heard that she'd be available soon. I thought we had more time, so didn't have anything for her yet. Well, except for the nanny. I made sure I had the best one in New England on retainer as soon as I even considered marrying Roger."

"How does he feel about the adoption?"

"Oh, he's over the roof with joy. He's the greatest uncle in the world to his sister's two boys. At first, I thought we were going to have to wait until a baby boy became available, but Roger said he'd always wanted a daughter. I guess the stars are aligning for us now…"

"Funny, I was thinking the same thing just a few minutes ago. So, tell me; you said this baby became available suddenly. I thought waiting lists were years out."

"Well, they are," the woman said, then dropped her voice to a whisper, forcing Chuck to lean close to hear her, "unless you know the right people. Or rather, the right doctor. We're paying over $50,000 plus expenses for this child. He's making a mint off delivering white babies to desperate folks like me. He has a few birthing homes stashed around the country, I hear."

"Can you tell me his name? This little girl might want a sister," Chuck asked, curious about the black market for white babies.

"It's some odd Indian or Pakistani name: Jeet or Peet or something like that. We just call him Dr. Buddy. His latest client is having triplets, but he's only making money on two of them. Apparently, the person who brought him the mother gets the runt of the litter. I'm getting the biggest one, he said. Since there's no guarantees, she'll have a better chance of survival. All the post-care is up to me. He's an obstetrician. As he's so fond of saying, 'I just pull them out. After that, the kid's all yours and the pediatrician's.'"

Gloria picked out a frilly pink dress, then set it back. "Maybe later. My sister-in-law said to keep away from ruffles and lace until they're older. It just scratches and itches their tender little skin. She's so excited about this baby. When she found out there was an extra one to adopt, she wanted her. But she was too late. That would have been so awesome: identical cousins."

"I'm sorry. I'm not following you," Chuck said, forcibly scowling in confusion to cover his ire.

"You see, the babies are identical! Three identical little girls…" Gloria sighed, her smile of contentment stealing any more words.

"Maybe you can find out who the other parents are. You know, keep in touch to see how much the girls look and act alike over the years."

"I'm one step ahead of you. I'm pretty sure I know who the one parent is. Luther has been a friend of mine for years. He and his wife Leanne have been wanting children for ages. He's some world-famous botanist, frustrated that he can get corn to grow on a rock but can't do anything about his wife's infertility. Yes, I'm sure they'll be great parents, too."

"How about this?" Chuck said, intentionally shutting off the thread of conversation by showing her a soft cotton sleeping gown. He already had the full name of one parent and enough information about the other adoptive family to get their last name. Not that he wanted to take the girls away from their new parents, but it would be nice to confirm that they were safe and loved.

A salesclerk followed Gloria around as she selected clothing and accessories while Chuck investigated the other side of the store, trying to keep the chitchat to a minimum. He didn't want to seem too curious, even though he did want to know what she knew about the person getting the 'finder's fee.'

He set three boxes of diapers and a carton containing a small portable bassinette by the register, then toted around an infant car seat by the handle, using it as a shopping basket, tossing in assorted gowns, blankets, bottles, and cans of powdered formula.

"You might want a couple of these," Gloria said, holding up three different styles of pacifiers. "My sister-in-law says they're a lifesaver. You'd better get all three, though. No telling which one she'll prefer."

He added the trio to the rest of his bounty on the counter, then took one more look around the store. "Am I missing anything?" he asked the clerk.

She pawed through the contents, looking down at his choice of bassinette, then nodded. "Yup. Unless this is a plastic doll, I suggest baby wipes." She pointed to the display on the end cap. "Make sure you get the unscented kind. Oh, and have plenty of plastic bags on hand for disposal. Babies are little, but they make a big stink!"

"And distilled water," Grace said, coming up beside him. "You don't want to use tap water." She set her business card on the counter in front of him.

"I don't know who you are or anything about you, but I kind of have that zing feeling with you, Chuck. Stay in touch. And if there is anything you need, let me know. I don't know when our little girls are going to be born, but it sounds as if they might wind up being zodiac twins."

"Gloria, I didn't say this was my baby. I'm not even married," Chuck said, adding a wink.

“If she’s not yours, you want her to be. Whether you’re Daddy or Uncle Chuck, there’s no doubt in my mind that you already love her.”

“That’ll be $374.36, sir,” the cashier said.

“It’s on me,” Gloria said, handing the clerk her gold charge card. “Her first gift from her silent godmother.”

Chuck took a deep breath, then bent forward and hugged the generous woman, ending his thanks with a firm kiss on the cheek. “You’re going to be a great mother, too,” he said. “Thanks for giving that little girl a good home.”

“My pleasure,” she said, tears welling. “My pleasure.”

Chapter 13
Arrivals

January 3, 1992

Cups and plates skittered across the room as Grace threw another tantrum, a spoon ricocheting off the TV stand and hitting Chuck in the head.

"Oh, God! I can't take it anymore! I'm serious," she cried, wiping her runny nose on the shoulder of her hospital gown, the only clothing that fit her. "Nothing is helping anymore!"

"Well, it looks like it's a good thing we cut you off from forks and knives," Chuck said as he cleaned raspberry jam from his forehead with a found napkin. He rose from the recliner that had become his domicile and office after he added obstetrician and nurse maid's duties to those of best friend. The oversized and overstuffed chair was his bed, dinner table, and research library.

"Are you done yet or have you found something else you can throw? Earrings, underwire bra, false teeth?"

Grace blanched as Chuck wiped the red stickiness from his head, then realized it was jam. She still felt bad for having struck him, even if unintentionally. "I'm sorry, Chuck. You've been a positive saint about all this. Scratch that. I think saints should take lessons in patience and sacrifice from you. I'm serious, though. Can we get the babies out now? They're big enough, aren't they? I overheard one of the nurses tell Buddy that the test results said the lungs were functional."

"You did? When was that? He didn't say anything to me."

"I overheard him the day before yesterday. He thought I was still sedated. He seemed really excited, too, when he looked at the sonogram measurements. He babbled something about 2200 something or other, and then I was out again."

"Grams?"

"Yeah, that's it," Grace said, then winced as a spasm hit. "He said they should all be over 2200 grams now. Does he mean that's how much they weigh?"

"Maybe." Chuck hit the volume up button on the TV remote and grabbed Grace's hairbrush. "Here, let me fix you up a little." He leaned close to her ear and whispered, "Yup, he's been keeping data from me. I'm pretty sure this room is monitored. I don't think he wanted you to know that they were ready to be born. I'm sure it's to keep you calm. Your blood pressure is still pretty high."

Grace turned toward him and gave a quizzical look. "What is it you're not saying? Are you worried about something?" she asked, her eyes shifting back and forth indicating their whole environment.

"Hey, Grace. Remember, as long as you have me, you'll be fine. Now, are you ready for this? It's too risky for you to deliver naturally. Lots of women would be jealous of the fact that you don't have to go through labor. Buddy has it under control, I'm sure. I've checked everything out and he has a fantastic operating room and neonatal clinic." *I just hope his postpartum recovery program is as great.*

Knock, knock, knock.

"Greetings and good day to you both," Buddy said, his teeth shining bright with a wide smile. "Are you ready to deliver?"

"Duh! I was ready two months ago, but I guess the question should be, 'Are the babies ready to deliver?'"

"Yes," Buddy looked down at the clipboard he held close to his chest, "according to the information from the last ultrasound and amniocentesis, the babies have attained a healthy weight and their lungs are fully developed."

He paused, looking at the scattered dishes on the floor, the oatmeal trail ending at an upside-down bowl. "So, how much breakfast did you eat today?" he asked, stifling a smirk.

"I didn't," Grace said with a pout of embarrassment. "Sorry about the mess. I had a bad night."

Buddy raised one eyebrow and looked at Chuck who replied with a shoulder shrug. He added, "She has a hard time sleeping.

Considering all she's been through lately, I'd say the damage is minimal. And yes, unless she has a pizza under her pillow and has been sneaking bites of it, all she's consumed in the last twelve hours was a little jello last night and water. She's ready for surgery and so am I. I'd still like to assist."

Bottom lip stuck out in thought, Buddy paused then nodded. "Yes, I think I could use an extra pair of hands. Grab a cup of coffee and a bite to eat from the kitchen if you need to, then I'll meet you in the surgery in thirty minutes. I think you'll find everything you need in there."

"But…but…" Grace sputtered, her hand on Chuck's arm, holding him back.

"Hey, this is what you've been wanting, isn't it? I just need to eat a little breakfast, so I don't get the shakes or pass out. Someone should be coming in to scrub you up a little, and then roll you down the hall to the operating room. By lunchtime, you'll be able to see your toes again. Tonight you can sleep, and by summer, you'll have your bikini-beautiful body back, your thin little cesarean scar invisible to onlookers."

"And all these stretch marks?" she asked, frowning.

"Believe me, those are minimal," Chuck said. "If they're even visible at all in six months, they'll just be little silver threads. Most women develop them at some time in their lives anyhow."

"And many men," Buddy added. "You probably just never looked. If they bother you, wear a one-piece suit. One last time, you do want to give up these babies up for adoption, correct? And you still don't want to see them or know their gender?"

Grace nodded as the tears fell again. "Damn! How long until these pregnancy hormones get out of my system? I've cried more in the last month than I have in my whole life!"

"A month or two. Give it time. Eat plenty of fresh vegetables and fruits, drink lots of water, exercise more than you thought possible, and you will have a speedy restoration to your pre-pregnancy body and attitude. Don't skip any of those, though, or depression will try to steal your life. I have medications for that, but good body maintenance works best." Buddy patted her on the shoulder. "Leave it to me and your friend. Chuck has your best interests at heart."

Chuck flipped his wrist, checking his watch. "Gotta jet, Grace. I'll be back in a flash. Don't go anywhere without me."

"Yeah, right, said the Galapagos tortoise to the Arizona jackrabbit. Have a good breakfast."

Chapter 14
Road Trip

January 3, 1992
Armstrong Estate, Massachusetts

"I found him!" Silas shouted out as he walked through the front door, fist-pumping the air in victory.

"Him? You mean them?" Papa Doc asked. "Chuck and Grace?"

"Nope, him as in Dusty. Damn! I know if Grace knew I found her old beau, she'd come out of hiding. How many weeks until she's due?"

"You know as well as I do that she's still three weeks out," Hal said.

"Yeah, well, she is having twins," Papa Doc said, "so by my experience, she's about a week out. Chuck won't let those babies get too big. Two eight-pounders is more than enough for even a seasoned mother to carry and way too much for an eighteen-year-old heifer."

"Do not refer to my daughter as a heifer," Hal said, "but I agree. Can't we just haunt all the hospitals in the area?"

"I've been doing that ever since they disappeared," Silas said. "I'm expanding the area now, just in case they migrated north or south."

"Who'd want to go north in the winter?" Hal asked. "No, wait. It doesn't matter. Sometimes I don't even know why we bother to look."

"Because she's our daughter and those are our grandchildren she's carrying," Papa Doc said. "And don't even think about contesting Silas's interest in her. Even if they aren't Alex's babies, I can't help but think of them as my grandchildren, too."

"Yeah, well, I'm more than happy to share the grandpa duties with all of you," Hal said. "These babies may not have a grandma worth claiming, but they'll make up for it with a bounty of grandpas."

"So, tell us, Silas, where's Dusty now, and where has he been hiding all these months?" Hal asked. "I never knew the kid beyond seeing him work with his father cutting grass or trimming hedges, but he seemed decent enough."

"So, you knew he was your landscaper?" Silas asked.

Hal nodded. "Yeah, for the last few years or so."

"Well, that would have been a good thing to know and might have made my search a lot easier. Or not. Anyhow, that's what he's doing now."

"It's winter! How in the heck is he a gardener now?" Hal asked.

"I'll let you ask him. He's clearing the drives as we speak. I told him to come up to the big house to get paid, that I had a bonus for him if his work was better than the last guy's."

"How much does he have left to plow? Do you think we should ask him to dinner? Does he know that Grace was staying here until last month? Oh, good grief! Does he even know she's pregnant? Shoot! Speak up, Silas," Papa Doc said. "Inquiring minds want to know!"

Hal and Silas burst out laughing at Doc's blathering and frustration. "I guess it wouldn't hurt to set another plate out."

"It's a good thing we're having chili and cornbread tonight. Plenty to share," Doc said, grabbing another place setting. "So, are we telling him about the babies or just pretending Grace has been hanging out here for the heck of it?"

Suddenly, Papa Doc and everyone else was silent, totally at a loss for words or sassy remarks.

Ding! Dong!

"I'll get it," Silas said. "You two do the talking. I did my part in finding him."

"I'm beginning to think he had the easy part," Papa Doc whispered to Hal.

"I agree. Toss you for it – loser gets the dishes." Hal flipped a coin. “Call it.”

“Heads.”

“Heads it is,” Hal said. “That means I lose and have to wash the dishes.”

“You mean, you win and get to wash the dishes,” Papa Doc groaned.

“Oh, Mr. Stillwater! Good evening,” Dusty said with genuine shock and enthusiasm, his hand reached out to shake his. “You’re the last person I expected to see.” Dusty suddenly blushed and became tongue-tied. “I…um…was wondering, how’s your daughter? I mean, I haven’t seen Grace in nearly eight months. Her mother said she was mad at me and never wanted to see or hear from me again…”

“She what?” Hal bellowed.

“I win twice,” Papa Doc whispered, then sat back and smiled, curious about how Hal was going to handle the explanation.

“Mrs. Stillwater was insistent that I keep away from Grace. I think she felt kind of bad about it. I mean, I think she knew how fond I was of Grace. She even gave me a ten-thousand-dollar check to use toward college so I could get a better education and maybe start a new life! For some reason, though, she thought I would do better if I moved to the west coast… Anyhow, I felt bad about taking her money, so I just held onto it. Plus, there was no way I was going to move so far away that I’d never see Grace when she was out and about. I mean, if I could just see her and talk to her now, I know I could make everything right.”

“So, what *have* you been doing?” Hal asked, stalling for time.

“Well, I really didn’t want to go to college, but I wasn’t going to take your wife’s money if I wouldn’t be using it for what she intended. So, I decided to use the check as collateral for a business loan. I bought a good used plow truck, a trailer, and some good second-hand mowers and gas-powered trimmers. I was right, too, about people willing to pay upfront for a contract to keep their driveways plowed in the winter and yards green and well-landscaped in the summer. I was able to pay back the loan in six months."

Dusty reached into his hip pocket and pulled out his wallet. "Oh, here. Please give this to your wife, sir. I got it back from the bank when the loan was satisfied."

Hal turned over the check, saw that it hadn't been endorsed, then verified the routing number. He took a deep breath, then decided to keep the fact that Dusty might have been in trouble if he had tried to cash a check on an account that Victoria had no legal rights to. "I'm proud of you, son," he said. "That was very clever, starting your own business like that. Um, I haven't seen Grace for quite a while. She took off on a… What would you call it, men? Maybe a journey of self-discovery?"

Silas and Papa Doc laughed nervously, glad that they didn't have to explain anything. "Yes," Silas said. "We haven't had any contact with her in quite a while, either."

"Well, I thank you for your business, Mr. Armstrong. I've heard good things about you. If you do hear from Grace, would you tell her I'd move heaven and earth just to talk to her for one minute." He paused, reflecting on what he had just said. "I'm serious. If I could just talk to her for one single minute, I'd give her everything I own…"

"No need to fret about that," Hal said, patting Dusty on the arm. "I tell you what, I'll make sure that as soon as we see her, we'll tell her she needs to talk to you. No ifs, ands, or 'I'm mad at him still's' accepted."

"I appreciate it, sir. Oh, and here's your invoice. I accept cash or check. I'm not set up for credit cards yet, but if you'd like to set up an account, I'll take you at your word and can send you a monthly statement."

"Yes, yes, Dusty," Papa Doc said, sniffing back tears of hope that there was still someone honorable and special waiting for Grace, even if it wasn't one of his 'good' sons. "If you'd consider me one of your regular customers, I'll breathe easier every snowfall."

"And summer? I still do groundskeeping. You can ask Mr. Stillwater here if he was happy with the work my father and I did."

"Most definitely consider us a year-round client," Papa Doc said.

Brrinng! Brrinng!

"Would you care to stay for some dinner?" Silas asked, picking up the conversation while Doc went into the kitchen to answer the phone. "Chili and cornbread. We're just getting ready to eat."

"I don't want to intrude…" Dusty paused, then sniffed the comfort food. "It does smell great, though."

"Just the right thing to warm your bones," Hal said, grabbing the extra place setting and arranging it next to his.

"Normally I wouldn't do this," Dusty said, "but I'm done for the afternoon. Plus, I skipped lunch."

"Coffee or hot cider?" Silas asked, holding up two carafes.

"Coffee, black, sounds good."

Papa Doc burst through the kitchen doors, excitement radiating from him like electricity from a three-foot plasma ball. "Hey, everyone. I hate to crash my own party, but we'll have to pack up this spread in to-go cups. We have to leave – like right now!"

"What?" Silas asked, setting down the coffee.

"We don't have a four-wheel-drive vehicle that will fit four, do we?" Papa Doc asked.

"You're talking crazy," Hal said. "What's going on?"

"That was Chuck. We have to go to New Hampshire and get Grace – and I mean right now!"

Dusty raised his hand like a first-grader eager to get his teacher's attention. "I have a four-wheel-drive crewcab truck outside. I fueled up just before I got here. Let me go, too, and I'll drive."

The older men looked at each other, each one nodding to the other. "Grab the coffee and some granola bars and let's go!" Hal announced. "My baby's comin' home."

***

Delivery/Operating Room, New Hampshire

"How are you doing, Dad?" Buddy asked.

Chuck grinned under his surgical mask, then realized Buddy couldn't see it. "Nervous as any other first-time father, I suppose. How'd she do?" he asked the anesthesiologist seated at Grace's head.

"She was a little nervous, but they all are. I made an excuse for your absence. If she asks, tell her you got over your stomach cramps; that it wasn't the flu." The bald and rotund knock-out specialist laughed. "Actually, I told her you had a sudden attack of morning sickness but not to worry. You'd be over it in nine months or sooner."

"How'd she take that?"

"Eh! Not too impressed, so I turned on the juice and let her sleep. She's young. She'll do fine."

Scalpel held up, Buddy said, "Here we go," then bent to his task.

Chuck had seen several cesarean section procedures, so knew what to expect. He was at the ready in case he was needed, but the surgical nurse was experienced and anticipated every clamp and suture Buddy needed. One, two, and the first babies were out, the two neo-natal nurses grasping their charges, then bringing them to the warming table to do their thing. Buddy maneuvered the afterbirth out of the way, then handed the last and smallest little girl to Chuck.

"She's small but viable," Buddy said.

Chuck glanced from his newborn to the doctor and saw an impossible-to-read expression in the Pakistani's dark eyebrows. "Thank you," he said sincerely, then took his daughter to the same neo-natal area, glad that he had taken time to make his phone call before the procedure.

Although the older nurse had given him a crash refresher course in post-delivery care of a preemie, his instincts took over as he did the quick assessments and ran through the procedures. Goosebumps rose at her squalls, verifying that her lungs were clear and working well. "Four pounds, eight ounces," he announced, echoing the brevity of the other nurses' announcements of five, six and five, eight. "In case anyone's taking notes."

"Nope," the younger nurse next to him said, then looked over to make sure Buddy was still concentrating on finishing up putting Grace back together. "This one's totally off the radar. As far as anyone knows, she had twins." She paused, waiting for Chuck to look at her. Seeing his eyes, she shoved her mask down with the back of her glove and mouthed, 'We need to talk,' then slipped the mask back in place. "Congratulations, Dad," she said aloud. "She's definitely a keeper."

***

"How soon can Grace be moved to the post-care apartment?" Chuck asked Buddy as they cleaned up and changed out of their scrubs.

"Soon, very soon. I've found it's better if they come out of anesthesia in a different environment. I make sure they're comfortable. A nurse is with them when they wake up to take care of any complications and make sure they have food and aren't alone. After that, it's up to them when to leave. Most don't stay around more than a day. As soon as they can walk, they've called a friend or family member, and then they're back into their lives as if nothing happened."

"Do they ever come back?" Chuck asked, concern furrowing his eyebrows. "I mean, do you ever deliver the same woman more than once?"

"No, but then I've only been doing this for a year. If you're interested, I can set you up." Buddy put his hand on Chuck's. "I know it didn't work out between the two of us on a personal level, but we could be business partners. You're already a physician with a wonderful bedside manner. That's so important, that the girls trust you. It's so easy to find rich wannabe parents, willing to pay anything to have a healthy white child. There are plenty of babies coming from overseas, but they're usually Asian. White parents want white babies; it's as simple as that."

Chuck swallowed back his disgust and faked a smile of interest. "I'll have to get back to you on that. I need to make sure Grace gets back to her family. If you don't mind, can I ask one of the nurses to keep an eye on my daughter for a minute while I check on her?"

"I don't mind at all," Buddy said, a sly smile arising. "There are two; take your pick."

Chuck approached the nurse who had given him the non-verbal warning, certain that she would help him and be discreet. Plus, a little alone time would give her a chance to speak with him. "Hi, I guess you already know my name is Chuck. I was wondering," he said, his eyes looking around the room to let her know he hadn't forgotten their interaction, but he needed to wait a bit for that, "if you could watch my daughter while I check on Grace."

He smiled as he said the words 'my daughter.' "I never thought I'd have a child. Do you know how wonderful it is for a gay man to be able to say, 'my daughter'?" he asked.

"Not the gay man part," the nurse said, "but I know about having a daughter and how good that feels, even if she was only alive for a short while. Sorry, we haven't been introduced. My name is Grace, too."

"Grace Two? That makes it easy for me. Well, Grace Two, would you watch Rhianna for me?" nodding to the smallest of the babies, now topped with a white knit cap, swaddled in pale yellow flannel.

"Nice to officially meet you." She reached out and shook his hand, pressing a small slip of paper in his at the same time, a slight frown of admonishment to be discreet marking her otherwise unreadable features. "I'm pretty sure I can look after two babies at the same time. Ellen has Baby One under control," she said, canting her head toward the hefty, older nurse beside her.

"I'll be back in a jiff, Grace Two," he said with a wink.

"Sure 'nuff," she replied. *Just read the note before you get back.*

Chuck pushed through the doors, his smile of joy shining for the security cameras that he was sure were everywhere. He ducked into the bathroom and into the shower stall, verifying that there wasn't a spot where a camera could be hidden. As an extra measure of privacy, he turned on the hot water, letting a cloud of steam form before he took out his note.

They're taking her to 11348 Mountain View after you see her. Have her picked up ASAP. Babies are getting moved soon. Take yours and scram!

Chuck collapsed against the shower wall, then slumped onto the shower seat, still fully dressed. He looked at the note again, then stuffed it back in his pocket. He pulled out his phone and texted his father again, this time with the new address.

"Are you all right?" Buddy hollered from the outer bathroom area.

"Yeah," Chuck replied. "I just needed a little shot of steam. You know, dry winter air and all. I'll have to remember to pick up a humidifier."

"How's Grace?" Buddy asked, his eye twitching and smile uncertain.

"Don't know yet," Chuck said as he walked up to him. He patted Buddy on the back. "I didn't want to greet her with a stuffy nose. She's probably still unconscious anyhow. Thanks for helping us out. Life is sure going to be different as a father, but it's a journey I'm looking forward to. I have to make sure Grace is set before I leave, though. Where did you say she was going?"

"She'll wake up completely at the apartment we keep in Skyline. I never send mail there but it's right on the corner of Oak and Main," Buddy said.

"Just making sure," Chuck said. "If Rhianna's still stable, I'm going to head out after I see how Grace is doing. Goodbyes are hard enough for me. I don't think I'll be able to tell her that this is goodbye forever. After she gets to the Skyline apartment, would you tell her I had an emergency or something? After a few weeks of not hearing from me, she'll figure it out."

Buddy breathed a visible sigh of relief. *Great! No interference from best friend!*

The change in attitude confirmed what Chuck had suspected. *Liar! You were planning on hiding her from me. Now, you're relieved that I won't still be glued to her elbow!*

"Yes, if she wants to stay in this part of the country," Buddy said, "I have a very good friend at an employment agency. I'm sure he can find something for her."

"Thanks again," Chuck said, then rushed out the door and into the hall before he threw up.

Pausing at the water cooler to compose himself, Chuck slowly sipped a cup of plain hot water. *Be strong. The dads will be there for her. I know they will. This is what's best for her.*

He tossed the paper cup in the trash and braced himself for one of the hardest tasks in his life: saying good-bye.

"Hey, Grace," Chuck said, standing beside her gurney.

Grace remained motionless as she feigned being asleep. The sense of immense loss was something no one had warned her about. The constant kicking and change of pressure on her internal organs were missing. The new stillness was as scary as a sudden loss of sight or hearing. Those uncomfortable and unpredictable sensations she had endured for the last six months were gone, never to be recovered – their memory, too intense to be forgotten.

"It's going to be all right, Grace," Chuck whispered, then sat next to her, his hand gentle on her shoulder. "I feel like a coward, but I'm afraid every time you see me, you'll remember this, these last few months. I told you that I'd always be here for you. Now, it's by leaving that I'm doing you the biggest favor. You're stronger than you know; braver and more generous than anyone I've ever met. Keep being you and you'll conquer this world and all the evils in it. I do love you, Grace. You've been the biggest, brightest star in my life. And you've given me more than I ever thought possible."

Chuck stood up, then bent over her and kissed her on the cheek. Tears had left a shiny trail from the corners of her eyes down her temples and into her hair. "Good-bye, my sweet. And good luck."

Rushing out the door, Chuck was hit with nausea again. *Coward! You can't turn around and steal her away now. Don't chicken out and do the easy thing. She needs to be free. She can't – won't and didn't – change her mind. Seeing Rhianna would tear her up. She's out of your life now. All you can do is make sure she's safe.*

"Oh, there you are," Grace Two said, halting her nervous pacing when she saw him walk back into the neo-natal area.

"Sorry, it took longer than I thought. I…um…ran into Buddy and we had a little chat."

Grace Two's eyes widened but Chuck's minimal head shake settled her fear. She looked to Ellen. "Can you watch all three for a minute? I want to go outside for a smoke."

"No problem. I'll let you spell me when you get back," the other nurse said. "Not for a smoke, though…"

Chuck's new confidant took him by the elbow and ushered him down the hall and out an exit. She glanced around, verified they were alone, then whispered, "There's going to be a bust here by morning. I talked the feds into waiting until these babies were delivered and had a few hours to adjust before whisking them away. They're all fine, but Buddy's going to get arrested for white slavery and a few more charges. He was going to use your Grace for breeding stock."

"What?" Chuck squeaked, quickly bringing down the volume as the word escaped.

"Surrogate mother. She's proven she can carry three babies and deliver them at a viable weight. Lots of rich couples are eager to have their fertilized zygotes implanted. Buddy will keep her around to recover as long as he can, ply her with a high paying, low skills job; then whisk her off to his birthing house. White slavery still exists. I want to end it right now."

"How do… How do you know this?" Chuck asked.

"I was one of them. He trusts me. In reality, I was just waiting until I could gain that confidence so I could bring him down. You're different. You were doing this for her, to get her out of a bind."

"Wait. The babies…"

"He's going to whisk them off and 'resell' them several times over. The promised parents will be told the babies died, that their fifty grand purchase price for a baby is non-refundable."

"I'm going to make a call," Chuck said, his hand on her shoulder – his emotional grounding rod. "Do you think you can help me get all these babies out of here? I have a van all set up for one baby. I think they'll all fit in the one bassinette, though. At least, until we can clear ground zero."

Grace Two looked at her watch. "He takes off to be with his wife at the big house at seven every evening, come rain, shine, or blizzard. If you can have your vehicle here and warmed up ten minutes later, we should be able to stay out of the shit storm. What about your Grace?"

"Buddy has a wife?" he gasped. "That explains a lot. Anyhow, her ride's already enroute. I just texted the new address to them. I hope the message comes through in time. They're driving up from Massachusetts."

"Well, make your other call fast then come in. He's going to suspect something if you're not spending every moment you can with your baby. Oh, and cell reception is best up there," Grace Two said, pointing to a cleared area at the end of the patio. "And no cameras."

Chuck took his cellphone out of his pocket as he walked away, glad that he had taken the time and expense to buy one. He took the business card out of his wallet and dialed.

"Hey, Gloria. This is Chuck. From the baby store. You're my daughter's godmother, remember? Yeah? Really? Mine was, too. No, she didn't die, too. They're all fine. Shoot. I suppose there's no holding back. Our daughters are sisters. At least, they're biological sisters. So, here's the deal. You need to be at the gas station on Sherlock and Hemingway at seven twenty tonight. I don't care if you're in the middle of the biggest dinner party in the world…well, it's a good thing you're both home. Anyhow, you and your botanist friend who has dibs on the other baby need to come and grab your daughters then. No, I promise you they're not dead. They're all perfectly healthy. Well, don't let Buddy know I called you. I think he's in big trouble. Yeah, well, telling you the babies died should be enough for you to doubt everything he says. I'll be in a plain white van – you know, the kind electricians use? Yeah, well it's a conversion. I'll have all the babies with me. Just give me the password 'Woodstock' and either I or the nurse will let you in. All right. Bundle up and bring car seats. I only have the one you bought for Rhianna."

"Rhianna," Gloria mused as she set down the phone. "Well, they both can't have that name. We'll have to find a different one. Roger!" she called upstairs. "Come on down. You got that miracle you were praying for. Let's go get her!"

"She's alive?" the red-eyed man asked, sniffing back leftover tears as he rushed down the stairs.

"Yup. You got me convinced that prayers work. Grab your coat and warm up the car. I'm calling Luther and Leanne and giving them the good news, too. I'm sure glad we left the car seat and welcome home goodies where they were. We're less than an hour away from holding our baby."

Chapter 15
The Shit Storm

Enroute to save Grace
January 3, 1992

"You know, a lot may have gone on during the last few months, Dusty. It's been how long since you've seen her?" Hal asked.

"It's been two-hundred-thirty-three days, sir. Sorry. I'm a little obsessive about the loss."

"Well, it's been a month and a day since we've seen her. All was fine and dandy at breakfast, then the next thing you know, she and my son had disappeared. Poof!"

"Um, Mr. Armstrong. I don't mean to sound rude," Dusty said, his foot off the accelerator as he thought of how he should word his concern without losing his new customer. "But don't you think it would have been a good idea to tell me that my girlfriend ran away with another man? You made it seem like…"

"Excuse me, son," Silas said. "We're in a hurry here. If you can't put the pedal to the metal, pull over and let me drive. Don't worry about Chuck. He's *Doctor* Armstrong's youngest son. He's a doctor, too. He's the one who's been taking care of her."

"Are you sure they didn't fall in love or something?" Dusty asked. "I mean, she's a wonderful woman, and beautiful, too."

"Pretty sure," Papa Doc said.

Silas leaned over and whispered, "Plus he's gay."

"He is? Oh, thank heaven!" Dusty blurted out, his foot now heavy on the accelerator. "I mean, that's good for me. And for her, too. I hope."

"And him eventually," Papa Doc added, comforted by the pat on the shoulder by Hal.

"So, Dusty, I don't mean to be a downer," Hal said, "but she has been gone for a long time. Would you still love her if she, say, gained a lot of weight?"

"Mr. Stillwater, I'd still love your daughter if she was a deaf-mute quadriplegic."

"And what if she committed a crime like maybe stole something big?" Silas asked.

Dusty sighed deeply, his foot coming off the gas again.

"Keep up your speed, son," Silas warned.

"Oh, yes, sir. Sorry about that. You see, though, she already is a thief. She stole my heart. She's who I think about when I fall asleep at night, and my first thoughts in the morning are of her, too. We were going to get married. I mean, we hadn't set a date or anything, but we knew we wanted to be in each other's lives forever and ever."

"Sounds like someone's been watching too many animated fairy tales," Hal whispered to Papa Doc.

"I heard that," Dusty said. "But yes, I do believe in happy ever afters. I know not everyone gets one, but I know that if we can just talk for a minute, I can convince Grace that we can have ours. I'm on the right track with this new career. She can help me with it, doing the books and all. We can get our own little apartment to start with, then maybe save up enough money for a down payment on a…"

"Just drive," Silas said. "We all know what a happy ever after is. We're just as eager to find out what's happened in the last month, too."

"It's been nearly eight months for me, sir. I'm sure she's just as beautiful and sweet as ever, though."

"Anyone for coffee and a granola bar?" Papa Doc asked to redirect the conversation. "I didn't bring the chili. Not a good idea in close quarters, if you know what I mean."

"Granola bar and coffee sounds good to me," Silas said. "Why don't you pull over and I'll drive. Speed limits were meant to be flexible in extreme circumstances. I can drink and drive legally as long as it's coffee. Come on, kid. You've been working all day. You need to rest up at least a little so you're in top shape to see her." *And don't pass out on the spot when you see she's either pregnant or a new mother of twins!*

***

Three hours later

"Wake up, Sleeping Beauty," Hal said, nudging the dozing Dusty who had fallen asleep. "We're at the rendezvous spot."

"Huh? We're where?" Dusty looked around, blinking moisture into his eyes as he tried to figure out where he was and who these old men were. A smile erupted on his face, splitting his dry bottom lip. He licked it and brought his elation down to an earthly level. "She's here? Now? Where?"

"I guess they haven't got here yet," Silas said. "The text said he'd let us know when she was on the road. Whatever that means."

"What does that mean?" asked Dusty.

"If I knew, I'd tell you. Just keep your eyes open. Now, Dusty," Silas said, turning sideways in the seat to face the anxious young man, "she might look a little different…"

Hal and Papa Doc snickered at the same time, then brought their hands up to contain their explosive reactions to a very pregnant Grace looking a 'little' different. "Sorry," Papa Doc sputtered.

Dusty gulped audibly, then reached for the thermos of coffee and poured a splash into his cup. "There's a little left if anyone else wants some," he said. He gulped it down, waiting for more comments. When none came, he voiced his suspicion. "I'm beginning to think that you all know something big and don't want to tell me."

"Big?" Hal whispered, then Papa Doc started snickering again.

"So, what did she do, go on an eating binge and she's as big as a house now? You think that just because she got fat, I won't love her?" Dusty fumed. "Because that's what it sounds like you're trying *not* to say!"

Silas lay his hand on Dusty's shoulder. "You'd make a good investigator, son," he said. "Yes, we're trying not to tell you that she got big. Last time we saw her, she *was* big as a house. Well, not a real house, but so big she could hardly walk."

"But why would she keep overeating if she couldn't even… Oh, shit! Is she pregnant? Is that why she's so big? Is that why she ran away from me? She's having our baby and…"

Dusty stopped when he felt Silas squeeze his shoulder. "What? Are you doing that because I'm right or I'm wrong?"

"The last time we saw her," Silas said, his voice slow while he chose his words, "she was pregnant. Very pregnant."

"Well, we did have sex, so I guess that means using the pull method doesn't work…"

Hal harrumphed but didn't say a word.

"Sorry, Mr. Stillwater. I guess we were a little early on the honeymoon part, but we are going to get married. I promise you. If Grace will have me, we'll get married right away."

"A lot went on after you saw her last," Papa Doc said. "It seems she and my eldest son were sort of an item, so to say."

"What? But she loved me! I know she did!"

"Yes," Hal said, his indignation overridden by compassion for the confused young man. "And her mother forbade her to see you again, then set her up with a new beau. Sorry, Doc, but we all know it's true. Grace wouldn't have slept with Alex if her mother hadn't essentially blackmailed her."

"How could she blackmail her own daughter? Grace didn't have any money that Mrs. Stillwater couldn't have taken anyhow."

"She blackmailed Grace with you. She was going to have you and your father arrested for… Let's just say my wife was ready to make up false charges against you and your father that would have put you two in prison for a long time. Grace pretty much had to become intimate with a stranger to protect you. I believe that she did it out of love for you."

Dusty's face skewed up. "You mean she had sex with another man because she loved me? That is what you're saying, isn't it?"

All the men hemmed and mumbled, but it was Papa Doc who spoke up. "She may have been coerced into it, but she knew she could never go back to you. Not because of you but because of what her mother would do. She had to start anew. What she hadn't planned on was falling in love with my son, Alex."

"But you guys said he was gay – that she ran away with your son the gay doctor."

"No," Papa Doc corrected. "Different son."

"Okay. So, maybe the baby's his. I'll challenge him, though. Even if that isn't my baby, it's hers. We can bring him or her up together. Where is he? I want a duel or at least a chance to win her back."

"First off," Hal said, "whether she goes with you or not is totally her decision. At least, you say you love her no matter what."

"And second," Papa Doc said, "I wish there was a way you and Alex could duel or duke it out or just sit down and talk about it, but you can't."

"Why not?"

"Because he's dead," Silas said. He turned around and saw he was right to answer for Doc. His best friend was crying all over again, recalling the loss of his son.

"I'm sorry, sir," Dusty said. "Truly, I am. But I swear to everyone in this car, that no matter who's the father, I'll take care of both Grace and the baby."

"Babies," Hal corrected. "They're twins."

"What? I'm going to be the father of twins?" Dusty screeched excitedly, dropping his empty cup on the floorboards. "That's great! I mean, it might be a little crowded in my trailer for a while, but we can…"

"Hold on there, Champ," Silas said, physically holding the excited man down with a shoulder grip. "I don't think it's going to be that easy. If it was, Grace would have stayed where she was with us. And we wouldn't be making a middle-of-the-night exodus into New Hampshire based on one phone call and a couple of texts. Something screwy's going on. You and I and everyone else need to keep a level head. Let me take the lead on this. The worst thing you could do is burst out of this truck as soon as you see her, scaring the Bejesus out of her."

"Yeah, I guess you're right," Dusty mumbled. "Damn it."

***

"My van's warmed up and ready to go. Do you have a plan or am I just winging it?"

Grace Two looked up at the clock. "You're a little early, Chuck, but that might be a good thing. Do you feel that itchy, crawly vibe in the air?"

"Yup, that's why I buzzed out half an hour early to get ready. No telling if we'll get another opportunity." Chuck looked over at the three babies, their isolettes pushed together under the warming lights, their little bodies swaddled in pink, aqua, and yellow to tell them apart.

"Come look at this," he said, canting his head so she'd follow him as he walked to the tropical zone. "Do you have a place to go?" he whispered, "because I could really use your help with Rhianna."

"Do I have a place? No," she said softly. "But I'm always ready. All I ever need is packed in the gym bag I've been bringing into work with me for the last three years."

"How big's that gym bag?" Chuck asked, a twinkle in his eye.

"I always knew you were smart, Chuck. Yup. It's insulated, padded, and will work great for transporting them for a short distance."

"I wish I had thought of picking up some baby dolls at the mall when I was there. They had some little ones that looked so real…"

"What do you think is taking up space in my gym bag right now?" Grace Two said, then nudged him with her elbow.

Chuck took a deep sigh of relief. He raised an arm, ready to give her a hug of gratitude, then quickly redirected the movement to scratch his temple. *Cameras!*

"So, how about we see what's in the kitchen for breakfast," he said in a normal tone. "I make a great omelet."

She looked up at the clock. They had half an hour until Buddy was due to take off to see his wife. “Go ahead and start prepping. An everything-but-the-kitchen-sink omelet sounds great. Ellen’s due back from her break pretty soon.”

Chuck sang ‘Oh, what a beautiful morning’ as he strolled down the halls, pausing at the thermostat to check the temperature. Making sure his back was to the security camera, he surreptitiously turned up the temperature to high. He flipped the lights off in every room down the corridor before cranking up those thermostats and leaving, appearing to be energy conscious but actually trying to suck up as much juice from the electrical panel as possible. In the bathroom, he fumbled through the drawers, found and plugged in the two high-volume hairdryers, and set them to max heat. Leaving them running on the counter, he popped into the shower room and turned on the infrared heat lamp, then walked out, ready to start breakfast. How long would it take to shut down the thirty-amp breakers and which would pop first? He grinned. He didn’t care as long as they shut down in the next ten minutes.

“Mega omelets,” he said, acting engaged for the security cameras that were everywhere. He fished through the refrigerator shelves, looking for eggs, meat, onions, and peppers for his supposed creation, adjusting the regulator to its coldest setting as he pushed aside different foods.

“Let’s see,” he said, thinking out loud. He pulled out two pans and set them on the stove, turning all four burners to high and cranking the oven to broil at the same time.

Grabbing a cleaver from the butcher block, he started chopping, making quick work of the ham, onions, and peppers. He glanced up at the clock. Less than five minutes. That ought to be enough time to pop a circuit breaker or two. Or set off a smoke alarm if something shorted out or caught fire. He cracked four eggs into the bowl, then bent over forward and clutched his belly. “Oh, no… Not again!” he said, then ran out of the room, leaving everything where it was.

Chuck pushed open the outside door and looked down the drive, making sure his vehicle was still running. That was the plus side to

Buddy being in an upscale neighborhood: no car thieves. Besides, who would want an old service van, even if it was four-wheel-drive and freshly painted?

The rumble of the garage door opening brought him out of his introspection. Watching from his secluded spot at the side of the house, he remembered to bend over and pretend to gag in case there were cameras he wasn't aware of. Buddy was pulling out, his white Cadillac squealing tires as it backed up hurriedly, as if he was late for an appointment.

"Crap!"

Chuck ran back inside, directly to Grace Two and the babies. He took a moment to catch his breath, one finger up asking her to wait a moment.

"Are you all right?" she asked, seeing that he was also flushed.

"Zero hour," he panted, then bent forward, this time truly ill but with nerves. "Get your bag. Stat."

The unlicensed but experienced neonatal nurse didn't waste a moment questioning him. She dashed down the hall, not concerned if she looked like she was crazy or not. It really was zero hour in more ways than one. She'd have her freedom, too.

As soon as she was back, her gym bag opened and ready, the lights went out with a *thunk!*

"Crap!" she huffed.

Chuck shined a flashlight on her bag. "Need a light?" he asked.

"Yeah," she said sarcastically. "What did you do?"

"I overloaded the circuits to give us a little element of surprise," he said. He squatted down beside her and helped her rewrap the dolls in the babies' spare blankets.

"Here," she said, pulling out a drawer under one isolette, handing him a fistful of knit caps. "We have lots of them."

Chuck finished dressing the dolls, then joined her at the warming station.

"I need light," she said, fidgeting with the babies under the glow of the battery-operated emergency light mounted in the corner of the ceiling.

He shone his flashlight on the little girls. She had already moved them to one isolette, the bassinette's thin bedding folded up around them like a taco shell. He held the bag open, the flashlight in his mouth showing her the spot to settle them in. The shuffling around had upset them, their little squalls now drowned out by the sudden blare of smoke alarms.

"Overloaded the circuits?" she repeated as a question.

He took the flashlight out of his mouth. "And I may have left a few burners on high without anything in the pans." He sniffed the air. "Pee Ew!"

"Ready, Dad?"

"Which door?" he asked.

"You take the babies. I know the secret exit."

Chuck wiped the flashlight off under his arm, handed it to her, then took the bag. "At least, we know we won't be running into Buddy. He already split. He left early and seemed to be in a hurry."

Grace Two shone the light on the floor, leading him in what felt like the wrong direction "That must be why I felt the tension in the air," she said. "He probably got a heads up. Damn!"

The two plus the babies wound up exiting where he had just experienced his pretend stomach distress. "There's the van." He looked to the right. "Uh, oh. We'd better jet. Looks like we have incoming…" he said, and scurried down the rise, leading the way.

"Quick," she said. "Give them to me, then you jump the fence."

"What?"

"It's only three feet high. Shit! Just step here…" She stepped on the well-hidden but strategically placed cinderblock next to the stucco perimeter fence, sat down and swung her legs over, stepping on another block before hitting the ground. "Give them to me, then you come over."

Chuck repositioned the strap and holding the babies close, was up and over the fence in a flash. "Got it. Sorry. I'm a little possessive."

"No worries, Dad," she said. She took two steps, then put up her hand, stopping him.

"Is everything all right there?" a voice called out.

"Yes, sir," Chuck answered. He squinted to see who it was, then put his arm around Grace Two's shoulder and pulled her close. "We're eloping!" he declared to the man in the FBI jacket. "Do you need to see ID?" he said, fumbling in his pocket, his smile wide.

"Heading out at this time of night?"

"Yes, sir," he replied. Chuck held up the gym bag and pointed to the van, obviously warmed up. "We were just staying with some friends on our way cross country. It's another three days to Vegas, but we were hoping to make the Lincoln Memorial by morning."

The officer looked at Chuck, all giddy with excitement, not nervous and scared as a white slaver would be, then made the snap decision to let them go. They'd just slow him down with paperwork.

"Have a safe trip," the FBI agent said. "And don't gamble!"

"Hey," Chuck quipped. "I can't say that! I'm getting married, aren't I?"

"Well, then, be safe."

"Thanks, we will," Chuck said, then gave Grace Two an extra squeeze of joy at their second victory: deception.

The two took their time walking the rest of the way to the van, holding hands, swinging them back and forth like schoolchildren to perpetuate the ruse. The joy was real. They were almost free!

Chuck unlocked and opened the side door, then handed her the bag. "Do you have this or do you want me to come back there and help you?"

"That might look a little suspicious. Even if it didn't, I want to get the hell away from here. Just watch out for bumps and sharp curves. I don't want to move them to the bassinette yet. They're snug and comfortable where they are."

"Kind of like they were still in the womb?" Chuck asked.

"Exactly."

"Then we're off to play stork to two very lucky couples."

"Honk, honk," Grace Two said, then chuckled. "I think I may like hanging around with you, Chuck. Just don't ever make a pass at me or I'll castrate you."

"Oh, me putting my arm around you and saying we were eloping?" he asked, suddenly concerned. "Is that what you mean? That was me insuring our exit. What were *you* going to do to get away? Bring out a shotgun?"

Grace Two grunted. "No. I'm sorry. If you can't tell, I've had a rough life…" She paused, then said, "Really. I'm sorry. I don't think I could have pulled this off without you. At least, getting these two to the parents. You did say they were good folks, right?"

"First, you can decide on whether you think they're good or not for yourself. We'll be meeting up with them in less than five minutes. Second, I'll never make a pass at you. Third, no further apologies or explanations expected or required."

"Got it." Grace settled herself on the bed, the babies in the bag held close to her midsection, her feet up, knees brought up around them. "Stork One, ready for takeoff."

Chuck checked his mirrors and put the van in drive. "Baby Drop gas station, here we come."

***

"Oh, my God," Dusty said, peering into the night. "Is that her?"

A matronly woman in a heavy winter coat had her arm around Grace, partially supporting her weight with her shoulder, an overnight bag dragging behind her. The *whoop! whoop!* sound of a cop car trying to get someone's attention frightened her, her head spinning like a demon as she looked to see where the sound had come from. Without a word, Nurse Ellen dropped the bag and ducked out from under Grace's shoulder, leaving her where she was, wavering in confusion.

The panicked nurse rushed back to the sedan and took off, tires spinning on the icy pavement. Left behind was a stunned and still semi-sedated Grace wearing a hospital gown, wavering in the snowy driveway with nothing but house slippers and a blanket around her shoulders to keep her warm in the sub-freezing weather.

"I ain't waiting, guys," Dusty said, and bolted out of the truck, hopping over hedges to get to her before she collapsed.

"I got you," he said. He wrapped the sagging blanket around her tighter, then held her close. Tears of joy streamed from his eyes at her nearness. He hadn't been able to see her face clearly in the dimness of the streetlight, but he knew it was her. He started to pick her up to carry her back to the truck but stopped at her yelp of pain.

"Are you okay?" he asked.

"No," she sobbed, leaning into his shoulder. She sniffed back the tears, then realized it was Dusty's scent, not Chuck's, that she smelled. "Dusty?" She blinked rapidly, lifting one hand up to wipe her eyes. "Is that you?"

"Yes, it's me, Dusty. I'll never let you out of my sight again."

Hal, Papa Doc, and Silas rushed over to join the reunion. "We got you, sweetheart," Hal said, crying just as much as they were, his arms wrapped around them both. "I promise, one of us will always be with you."

"But Mother…" she pined.

"Gone. Out of the picture. Divorce is in the works. I have some really stinky dirt on her now. I doubt she'll ever bother us again."

"But…but…they're gone. The nurse told me they died. They were fine at first, and then they died."

"Our babies?" Dusty asked. "They died? Both of them?"

Grace nodded, tears streaming, nose running, shoulders heaving, and without the energy to say another word.

"Let's go home," Papa Doc said, then moved in between Dusty and Hal to help bolster Grace. "There's plenty of room for all of us at the big house."

***

"Is that them?" Gloria asked her husband, clinging to his arm, tiptoeing to try for a better look.

Roger gave her hand a comforting pat, then moved away from the group so he could see the station wagon pull up to the gas pumps. “I don’t know. Did he tell you what he’d be driving?”

“Oh, yeah. He said he’d be driving a white van,” Gloria said. “Remember the password, ‘Woodstock.’”

“Sounds like my kind of guy,” Luther, the other father, remarked. He hugged his wife around the shoulders. “Remember when we were there?”

“How could I forget,” Leanne giggled. “Over twenty years ago, and now our baby is finally here. That’s a long gestation!”

“There’s Chuck!” Gloria exclaimed, hopping up and down with joy, her hands tucked under her chin at seeing his familiar face behind the steering wheel of the white van.

“Settle down,” Roger said. “You don’t want to bring attention to us.”

“Two middle-aged couples, snuggled up against the wind, looking like vultures ready to pounce… I’d say we were already suspicious,” Luther said.

Chuck looked beyond the gas pumps and saw the two couples standing by the stack of bundled firewood, their smiles of anticipation marking them as the new parents. He rolled past them and came to a stop at the side of the mini-store, out of sight of anything but owls searching for dinner. “Tranquility base: Stork One and Stork Two have landed,” he said, then opened the door and got out.

“Hey, there,” he said to the huddled foursome. “Anyone for a game of golf? Know a good course around here?”

“How about Woodstock?” Gloria said, then ran up to Chuck and gave him a big hug. “Are they inside? Are they okay? I thought I was going to have a total meltdown when Dr. Buddy called and said that Grace had died, and they couldn’t get the babies out in time. That they had all passed.”

Chuck’s eyes widened. “Grace was alive when I left.” He opened the side door, exposing his new traveling nursemaid and the gym bag full of babies.

“I’m still alive,” Grace Two said indignantly, then groaned

softly as she realized it was a misunderstanding about the shared name. “I think you’d better call me Nanny.” She looked at the eager parents, crowded around the open door, the women squeezed in front of their husbands to keep away from the chill. “Why don’t you ladies come inside?”

Gloria led the way. “Which one is ours?” she asked once inside, peering into the unzipped bag.

“It’s up to you two who gets Aqua and who gets Pinkie. The yellow-wrapped sweetheart is mine,” Chuck said, watching the allocation of babies from the front seat.

“Oh, my God!” Leanne exclaimed. “They are identical! I can’t believe it. How will we know whose is whose?”

Little Pinkie opened her eyes, started to squall, then caught sight of Gloria and smiled. “I don’t care if she’s the biggest or not; this one’s mine.”

“Then that must mean she’s ours. Oh, I can’t believe it. I swear I feel a tingling in my breasts. I’m as barren as a moon rock, but I swear she’s kicked in a bucket load of estrogen.” Leanne looked at Nanny. “Can I take her home now?”

“That’s the plan. Oh, and don’t even try to get in touch with Dr. Buddy. Either of you. If they didn’t catch him, they will. You’re lucky Chuck and I got in the middle of this or you wouldn’t be celebrating motherhood tonight.”

“Thank you, Nanny,” Gloria said. “Chuck has my number. If you two run into any trouble or need a few bucks, just give me a call.” She unzipped her jacket and put the swaddled baby inside. “Come on Vickie. You’re coming home.”

Leanne copied Gloria’s tactic of carrying the baby inside the coat. “And you, too, Tori Lynn. Daddy’s waiting outside.”

Leanne stepped out of the van, then suddenly yipped. “She latched on! Oh, my Lord! I’m going to see if Luther can set me up with some of those plant estrogens. I may be able to nurse my baby still! Sing hallelujah!”

***

"I need to get some fuel before we head out of town," Silas said. "I'll pull in up here. Anyone need anything?"

"Gracie, do you want something to eat or drink?" Dusty asked.

"Something to drink," she said. "Maybe water?"

"Get her some chocolate milk and pick up a gallon of water, too. She needs some calories and we all could use the water," Papa Doc said. "You go ahead inside." He reached in his pocket and pulled out a fifty-dollar bill. "Get whatever you want, too. I'll stay with her."

"But…" Dusty started to protest, then saw how Grace was snuggled into Hal. Right now, she needed her father more than anyone else. "Thanks, Doc."

Silas pulled into the gas station at Hemingway and Sherlock. It seemed busy, but then he noticed that the three vehicles weren't getting fuel but were having some sort of meeting at the side of the building. "Drug dealers," he muttered when he got out, then saw that the men huddled by the side door were older. "Just pot," he added with a chuckle, then turned away to fuel both tanks on Dusty's truck.

"Do you want a coffee, Silas?" Dusty asked. "Doc's buying."

"Sure. Black, no sugar. And get me the biggest chocolate bar you can find, too."

"Gotcha," Dusty said, then walked into the mini market, grinning wide in uninhibited joy at finally reconnecting with the love of his life.

***

"That went well," Chuck said after the two couples had left. "Are you ready to hit the road, Nanny? Hmm. I really do like that name. It fits you. No nonsense, but nurturing."

Grace Two, now renamed Nanny, couldn't help but smile. "New name, new beginning. Works for me. Did you remember to pick up distilled water for mixing the formula? I didn't see any in here."

"Oh, shoot! I'm glad you noticed. No, I forgot. I'll run in and get some right now. Do you want a soda or coffee or anything?"

"Coffee, black, would be great."

"I'll get you something else, too. Stress eats up calories and we have a long way to go," Chuck said, then mumbled under his breath, "Wherever it is we're heading."

Chuck walked in and looked around. "Where do you keep the water?" he asked the clerk.

"What is this? There's a real run on bottled water tonight. Back there. See that kid with the ball cap? Yeah, right next to him."

"Thanks. And is the coffee fresh?"

"Just made a pot. Don't tell me; you want a giant chocolate bar, too," the clerk said, adding a chuckle.

"Hey, that does sound good."

"Just follow the kid. He's after the same stuff."

Chuck went to the back of the store where the young man was and found the water. "Dang!" he said, checking the label, then noticed the kid had picked out a bottle with a different colored cap. "You got the last distilled water, didn't you?"

Dusty lifted up his jug of water. "Shoot. I don't want this kind. Here, I'll swap you. I was after spring water for drinking."

"Thanks," Chuck said, then headed to the coffee kiosk. "What did we do before convenience store coffees?" he commented.

"Shoot. I don't know," Dusty answered. "I don't think I was born yet. For me, they've always been around. I didn't even know what a rotary phone was until I was clearing out my dad's attic. I can't imagine having to stay in one room while talking, tethered to a six-foot curly cord."

Chuck blew out a breath, stopping short of a full laugh, and shook his head. "Yeah, our folks really had to rough it. Have a good night, what's left of it," he said and saluted the young man in farewell.

"Yeah, you, too," Dusty said. "I know it's going to get better because I just found my woman. Thank you, Lord!"

Chuck paid for the water, coffee, and candy then walked to the side of the building and rapped on the side door of the van. "What's the name of Snoopy's bird?" he asked.

Click.

Nanny opened the door and let him in. "Do we have to keep doing that?" she asked.

"No, probably not. I'm just trying to bring a little levity to this harrowing evening. I know my emotions are all over the place. Elation at getting out of there with all three babies alive; fear of either being caught by Buddy's crew or being charged as an accomplice by the FBI; excitement with being able to help two couples get the daughters they were told were dead; and absolute sadness and loss at having to walk away from Grace. Lord, I hope the guys got her. Oh, shit!" he said, his voice loud as if he'd just been pinched. "I can text them!"

Chuck pulled his cellphone out of his front pocket and tap, tap, tapped the quick message to his father. 'Did U get her?'

***

"Here you go, Mr. Stillwater," Dusty said, handing the gallon of drinking water and chocolate milk to Hal.

"Seeing as you've been through so much hell and still seem pretty set on marrying my daughter, you can go ahead and call me Dad or Hal, whichever feels more comfortable."

Beep! Beep!

"What was that?" Dusty asked, looking around.

"My cellphone," Papa Doc said. "I got what they call a personalized alert tone for my incoming texts." He took the phone out of his shirt pocket, tapped a few buttons, and then put it back in his pocket. He looked at Hal and grimaced. "Someone just checking to make sure all went well on our end," and nodded at Grace.

"It's going to take time for all of us to heal," Hal said. "Some losses take longer to get over. Let's hope you haven't lost Chuck because of all of this."

"Only for a little time. My son has a nurturing soul and is a gentleman. I think he's just stepping back so Dusty can help her heal."

"What do you mean? He didn't know Dusty was coming with us or that we even found him. That was last minute, remember?" Hal said.

"Yeah, I wouldn't know your son if I sat on him," Dusty said. "Hey, does anyone want some chocolate?"

Grace listened to the men banter back and forth, their voices rising and lowering with their emotions and concerns. She hadn't heard her father and two surrogate uncles in a month and didn't realize until now how much she had missed them. She looked out the window. The world was getting better, itty bit by itty bit. Dusty was here. Would he accept her as she was? The way he had held her – sobbing uncontrollably with joy – when he rescued her after she had been abandoned by Nurse Ellen, she knew he'd do anything for her. He seemed to be sharing her feeling of loss for the babies, too. All her men could mourn with her. And they would heal together, too.

All but Chuck. Where was he? She closed her eyes tight and tried to find a thread of recent memory, struggling to recall the last words he had said to her. There it was. An echo of his words. He was leaving her, he said – leaving so she wouldn't associate him with her loss.

Which would have been worse, the loss of the babies to adoption or death? Definitely death. With adoption, they would still have been happy little people with families who cared for and cherished them. Now with death, they were just little corpses. Was it her fault they had died? Did she do something wrong?

Grace looked at Dusty, blinking back the tears that had returned. A familiar movement out of the corner of her eye caught her attention. She leaned over him to watch the man coming out of the convenience store. "Who's that?" she asked, pointing out the window.

Dusty recognized him as the man he had swapped jugs of water with. "Just some guy from the store. He got coffee and water, too.

Why? Do you know him?"

She sighed then leaned back into his arm. "I thought I did…"

"Grace, I know it's not exactly romantic – my timing and all – but I want to make a new life with you as my wife. I have a lot going on now. I have my own business and everything. I still want to marry you and always will. We can start again with a family as soon as you say the word. I kinda know what went on with the other guy, and it doesn't matter to me. I mean, I know you have been hurt in about a million different ways, but I want to help you heal. Would you let me? I mean, I'd do it however you want, but I'd rather do it as your husband than as your best friend."

Grace leaned into Dusty and inhaled his unique scent of boy and man. She felt the first smile in ages come to her face. She looked up. "Yeah, I think I'd like you better as a husband. Let me get healed up, and then let's get married. But if you don't mind, I'd still like to live with Papa Doc and Silas for a while. And hang out with my dad, too."

"And me?"

"Duh! You'd be living with us, too. One great big dysfunctional family."

"With a live-in groundskeeper," Dusty added.

***

"One month today," Papa Doc said. "Do you think we ought to have a candle or something for this cake?"

"Nope," Silas said. "That's just calling attention to what happened a month ago. You can put sparklers on it, though."

"Why? What for?"

"I was going to let Hal tell you, but his divorce is final. I talked him into sharing the news with everyone at dinner tonight."

"Hey, there!" Grace said as she walked into the kitchen and gave both men a hug. "I was just wondering… And I want you to tell me the truth now. No sparing my feelings because if you do that when I ask a direct question, I'll take that as lying to me."

"Fair enough," Doc said. "Shoot."

"It's been a month since…well… I haven't heard from Chuck in a month. Have either of you? Or do you know of anyone who has? And that includes texts, emails, phone calls, or rumors of any or all of the above."

"Wow," Silas said, chuckling. "You don't give a creative guy any wiggle room for shaving warts off the truth, do you?"

"Answer the question, because by that answer, it sounds like you don't want to tell me something."

"Grace, if my son called, you'd probably hear me yell at him from here to Canada, giving him hell for ditching you. No. Not a hint, whisper, cyber-sent word or letter. I don't even know if he's dead or alive. I know that sounds harsh, but yes, I'm concerned. I have a bucket of hope that he's just giving you and Dusty time to get reacquainted and settled. Maybe he thinks if you see him, you'll remember all you went through together."

"Hmph!" Grace frowned, then turned to the other man in the room. "Silas…"

"Ditto what he said except I haven't been sitting around waiting for him to contact us. I've been scouring the east coast looking for him. I have his credit card info, and there's not so much as a five-dollar charge for a burger. He's gone dark. He's off the radar."

"And don't even think to say that he's dead," Papa Doc piped in, his voice high with protest. "If something bad happened to him, they'd notify next of kin, and that's me. Nope, that man could give a shadow hints on how to hide in a spotlight."

He came over to Grace and put his arm around her. "He's given you the gift of a fresh start. Don't stomp on it by looking for him. One of these days, he'll show up. Mark my words. I feel it in my bones."

"Me, too," Silas said. "And it isn't my rheumatism acting up, either. You and Dusty are doing great together. I appreciate you two hanging around here, but if you want to go somewhere to make a home of your own, let me know. I have a few bucks held back and I'm not bashful about sharing them with my adopted daughter and her husband."

"Here, here!" Hal said, popping through the back door and saluting the group with a bottle of champagne. "It's my emancipation day! The divorce is final! As a show of good riddance and thanks for not hanging around to make any more bad memories, I bought Victoria a one-way ticket – non-refundable – to Costa Rica."

"And she took it?" Papa Doc asked.

"All I had to do was wave a blank VHS tape in her face, the box marked 'My Good Times with André the Giant.' Man, I wish I had a picture of the look on her face!" Hal wrapped his arm around Grace's shoulder. "She's out of our lives for good. I am so, so sorry that I couldn't get rid of her sooner."

"Well, as my old friend PollyAndy would say, 'Better today than tomorrow.'"

"Come join us in a toast," Hal said when he saw Dusty walk in the door. "Here's to friends, family, and joyous tomorrows!"

"But, I'm not old enough…" Dusty stammered.

"No one's carding tonight," Silas said. "Cheers!"

"Cheers to all of us!" Grace said. "Happy Independence Day, Dad."

"And to all a long life!"

The End

Afterword

Would you like to know more about Chuck, Grace and Dusty, and all those wannabe grandpas? I intentionally went back in time to late 1991 and early 1992 to begin this saga. Soon – very soon – the triplets will all be grown up with love lives of their own! Here's a quick overview of the upcoming stories:

Vickie – Gloria and Roger's daughter – is dealing with lifestyles of the rich and famous in *Diamonds Aren't for Everyone*.

Rhianna and her healing-oriented beau who has *That Magic Touch* will be giving her dad – Chuck, remember him?

The Woodstock hippie botanists – Luther and Leanne – have their hands full with their spunky terror. *How Love Grows* follows Tori Lynn, an independent beauty who doesn't want to be taken at face value, as she tries not to fall in love with the new hand on her parent's marijuana farm.

The young woman Silas met at Woodstock in 1969 has shown up in his life again. Will they make a go of it? Will her secret ruin their possibility of a second-chance romance? *They Call Me Sherlock.*

Thanks for reading, and remember, authors love to get honest reviews!

About the Author

Author Dani Haviland started writing late in life and has been making up for lost time with a flood of works from sports, rom-coms, historicals, time travel, and Sweet and Sassy romances to Unforgettable romantic suspense and cozy mystery tales – with a few short stories thrown in to round out the reading experience.

Dani is also the owner of Chill Out! Books, one of the publishers for The Authors' Billboard. Follow her on Amazon and BookBub to make sure you get her latest stories.

Contact information:

Website: www.danihaviland.com
Facebook: Dani Haviland Author
Amazon Author Page: http://bit.ly/dhAuthor
BookBub: http://bit.ly/BBDani
Goodreads: http://bit.ly/2DHgdrds
Email: dani@danihaviland.com
Twitter: @dani_haviland, @gr8authors

I love to hear from readers!

Sign up for my newsletter to get the latest information on new releases, free stuff, and contests at: http://bit.ly/2DHnews

Other Books by Dani Haviland

ARLIE UNDERCOVER SERIES (romantic suspense based in Alaska and Arizona)

A Stingray Christmas: (First book) Anchorage detective on medical leave travels from Alaska to Arizona to see for the first time the son he'd fathered as an anonymous sperm donor. Great and rotten surprises await the cop with the smartest smartphone around.

The Biggest Heart Ever: (Book two) When would Arlie learn that trying to do everything by himself could be deadly—and make Charlene a widow before they were married?

Always a Bigger Fish: (Book three) Back in Alaska, Arlie finds out he's a target. Will vacationing detective Billy Burke (from THE FAIRIES SAGA) have information to help nab the scalper?

How to Fix a Broken Life: (Book four) When Arlie's very pregnant wife is kidnapped by pseudo terrorists, will he be the one to rescue her or will a surprise hero come in to save the day?

Because You Said So: (Book five) Something's amiss at the Port of Anchorage. Will Arlie be able to solve it and still be back in time to wear the Santa suit?

Heaven and Heartbreak: (Book six coming soon!)

TRIPLETS: THREE AREN'T ONE

The Set Up: (First book) Grace's story. How it all began with the mother from hell.

Diamonds Aren't for Everyone: (Book two) Vickie's story – Growing up a billionaire.

That Magic Touch: (Book three) Ria's story – Doctoring in the backwoods with secrets.

How Love Grows: (Book four) Tori's story – Growing up in vineyards and marijuana farms.

They Call Me Sherlock: (Book five) – Back to Woodstock with a friend.

THE FAIRIES SAGA SERIES (historical fiction/time travel, listed in order):

Kibbles and Bits: FREE ebook: Sample the first stories in the series before you buy. The Fairies Saga stories. Find out how the first five books got their crazy names, too.

Naked in the Winter Wind: (lengthy novel) How does an older woman wind up as a young hottie in Revolutionary War era North Carolina? First book in the time travel series.

Ha'Penny Jenny: (historical novella) More about the naïve and psychic young girl who was adopted into a time traveling family. Will her past catch up to her?

Aye, I am a Fairy: (lengthy novel) Young British lord finds himself entwined with a time traveling family and must decide if he should go back in time, too.

Dances Naked: (novel) Directionally challenged time traveler is rescued by Cherokee in 18th century. What must he do before the chief will show him to The Trees, the portal through time?

Chasing Christmas: (historical novella) A young Cherokee is rescued from an abusive man and changes the lives of many in this 18th century America family.

The Great Big Fairy: (lengthy novel) Very tall Benji grew up in the 20th century but was born in the 18th. When he finds a way to return to his grandparents in the distant past, he goes for it. Once there, he realizes he can't stay, but must return to the future.

Little Bear and the Ladies: (historical novella) What's a bachelor trapper to do with all the females he rescues from the Hessian mercenaries? He'd better hurry and figure something!

Little Drummer Boy: (historical novella) Young Scout works to earn money for a home in post-Revolutionary War America but runs up against prejudices and snowstorms.

Never Too Young: (historical novella) Scout and Ha'Penny Jenny have grown up, but will they be able to spend their life together, or will the past and ruffians get in their way?

Time in a Little Blue Bottle: (time travel 'mash up' novella) Elvis, Mark Twain, and the prime vampire are racing to get the bottle of Fountain of Youth water before sweet Bella and the youthful pickpocket. So why are time travelers Marty Melbourne and Master Simon interested?
Kidnapped!: Benji's sister has been abducted and he and his Scottish police officer brother-in-law will do anything to get her back...even trust the mysterious letter sent by an ancestor, a convict on The First Fleet into Australia!
Big Mac: Can Big Mac stop his sire, the errant Viking time traveler, from starting a pandemic?

CONTEMPORARY NOVELLAS – BENJI, THE LOST YEARS

Luke the Unexpected: Love of classic motorcycles brought them together, but Luke and Holly have other challenges to face. Find out how their friend Benji got his stripes here.

Pool Boy Wanted: No Experience Preferred: (rather racy) Young Benji has been a hostage and slave, but life gets worse when an older woman decides she wants him as her own.

STAND ALONE NOVELLAS (contemporary romances)

Kit Kringle: An Alaskan Tale: Kay moved to Alaska for the wrong reasons, then decided to stay and start her own business. What she hadn't planned on were prejudices and falling in love.

Be My Angel: Wyatt's dream to help save the wild mustangs began with the purchase of a rundown ranch in western Oregon. What he hadn't anticipated was being mesmerized by a sassy woman in a wheelchair.

Three Are One: The post chaplain tried to help the young widow adjust, but would his feelings for her and the search for his lost sister cause problems?

One Arctic Summer: That unforgettable summer of 1994 in Barrow, Alaska, and the touch she never forgot…If she goes back, will he remember her?

The Polar Xpress: Will the California chiropractor get a first chance at romance with the owner of Second Chance Kennels when he is stranded in Alaska?

Too Fast For You: Ten years after Little League, two talented professional baseball players wind up on the same minor league team. Will she remember him? And will their friendship be ruined if she does?

www.ingramcontent.com/pod-product-compliance
Lightning Source LLC
Chambersburg PA
CBHW061239170626
46809CB00007B/2750